One Taillight

By C.S. CROOK

Carolyn Sue Crook. One Taillight

ISBN-13: 978-1977839930

ISBN-10: 1977839932

When a convenience store is robbed and the young and beautiful clerk, 19 year old Cindy Porter, is abducted, residents on both sides of the Washington and Idaho state line fear the worst, because young women have been disappearing for years without a trace. Residents fear that a serial killer or killers are in their midst, and local law enforcement has been working diligently to solve the cases, but to no avail. The FBI had been assisting with the effort until, with mounting pressure from the residents in both states; they realize that they need to bring in their Special Tactics Team, led by Commander Chad Turner. He and his team are only deployed to seek out and bring in the most lethal predators.

Contents

Chapter 1

FBI Special Agent Chad Turner walked into the sheriff's office in the tiny town of Weaverville, which sat 70 miles to the east of the Washington State border. A potbellied gentleman in his late 50s pushed his chair back from a desk, stood up and asked, "May I help you, sir?" A dispatcher sat at a tiny desk in the corner of the room and had his legs propped up on an empty chair next to him. When the dispatcher saw Chad, he hurriedly placed his feet on the floor and straightened up in his chair.

"I'm Special Agent Chad Turner from the Federal Bureau of Investigation."

The potbellied man extended his hand to Chad and said, "I'm Sheriff Marker. We have been expecting you, and I can't begin to tell you how happy we are to have your help on this case."

Chad took the man's extended hand and shook it, "We're happy to be of any help that we can. What do you have to go on so far?"

Sheriff Marker said, "Not much, I'm afraid. We have a missing store clerk, a dead highway patrolman who stopped the clerk's car, and a grainy video from the convenience store where she got abducted from. Washington State police have triangulated her last cell phone activity, which came from their jurisdiction. Just before she got abducted, there were several vehicles seen in the area. We have been tracking down those leads, but we've hit a brick wall, I'm afraid."

"Do you have the video in your possession now?"

Sheriff Marker opened up a desk drawer and handed Chad a video tape wrapped in plastic and marked as evidence. "I hope you Federal guys can enhance that. It looks pretty hopeless to me. It is from a very old and out of date system. It is beyond me why store owners, who have their family members working those stores, are too cheap to put in good systems."

"Do you have photos of the missing subject?"

Sheriff Marker rummaged through some folders on his desktop, produced a file and handed it to Chad. Chad opened the folder and his heart sank to the pit of his gut. In the folder, an eight by ten picture of a bright eyed blonde girl smiled up at him. Her big blue eyes sparkled with the joy of life. She couldn't have been a day past eighteen years old. Sheriff Marker read the expression on his face and said, "She's just a kid. I knew Cindy ever since she was knee high to a grasshopper, which makes me hate this job. I always know them."

Chad looked up at him from the smiling girl in the photo and asked, "You get many of them here?"

"No, thank God for that, but when I do, it still hurts like hell. There have been quite a few in our surrounding counties though. Some of those girls have been missing for years. Your office clearly must think Cindy is one of the latest victims in those cases to send someone of your caliber here."

"It has not been established yet, Sheriff, that these cases are connected."

"Because none of them have been recovered, except for runaways?"

"That, and until we have a body, there is always hope the kid is still alive. But, if we do end up with a body, the way I look at this is we are in a unique position to do something about this, Sheriff Marker."

"You're an optimist I take it, Agent Turner?"

Chad looked him straight in the eye, closed the folder, and said, "No."

"What is your plan of action, Agent Turner, if you don't mind me asking?"

"First, I'm going to get our forensics team at the lab to try to enhance this video, and I have members of my team paying your neighbors a visit in Washington State. Their assignment is to see if we can't help them narrow down their triangulation of that last cell activity. If we can accomplish that, we will set up a search of the area."

"You're going to have a grid search done?"

"No, we will use scent hounds. If that turns anything up which is viable, we will expand to a grid search. Does the subject have any known enemies?"

"No, Cindy is a very well-liked and popular kid."

"Have all her friends and family members been questioned?"

"We've done a pretty thorough job of that."

"What about past boyfriends?"

"Yes, that is the first place we started."

"Good, then you won't take offence, if we start there too?"

"Not at all, I would expect it. We need to find the girl. Like I said, we welcome your help. I was sincere when I said that."

Chad studied the older man's face and said, "My team and I appreciate your cooperation. It makes all the difference in a situation like this, especially having someone who knows the local population the way you do, sir." Chad opened the folder again and found the address of the subject. "Did Cindy live alone at this address?"

"No sir, she lived there with her parents and siblings."

Chad scanned a fact sheet in the folder, which had a list of known male friends complete with addresses, and each had a check mark by their name. They were listed in order, with the current male friend Dale Summers at the top. Chad handed the sheriff a business card and extended his hand to Sheriff Marker. The sheriff took his hand

and shook it. Chad said, "It has been a pleasure to meet you, Sheriff, we will be in touch. I'm on my way to pay Mr. Summers a visit."

"We will let you know if we come up with anything else, Agent Turner."

"Thank you," Chad said and left the sheriff's office. When Chad returned to his car, he called and arranged to have a local courier meet him to pick up the tape. He instructed the courier to fly the tape out with the highest priority.

Next, Chad drove through the tiny town, until he found the home of Dale Summers. It was a humble clapboard sided house setting in a row of others just like it. A lifted Dodge Ram 4-wheel drive truck with oversized wheels sat parked in front of this particular one. Chad knocked on the door. A lanky young man with shoulder length black hair and a full beard opened the door. Chad flipped open his badge case and displayed it to Dale. Dale's eyebrows shot up in surprise. "You're from the FBI? They've got you guys working on this?"

"Are you Dale Summers?" Chad asked.

"I am. Hey look, I've already told our local yokels that I don't know anything about Cindy's kidnapping."

"Were you and Miss Cindy Porter having any disagreements that we should be aware of?"

"Hell no, we were tight! Look, you can ask anyone. She was crazy about me!" This time it was Chad's turn to raise his eyebrows. This was one arrogant young buck.

"Do you know of any other male who may have been paying undo attention to Miss Porter? Were there any stalkers, anyone making trouble or talking of making trouble, or just obsessed with Cindy's looks?"

"Well, there were always creepy regulars that came into the store." Dale held up his hands, making quotation marks in the air to emphasis regulars. "Cindy said the type which came in several times a day and bought little nothings. They just got off looking at her; they always creeped her out."

"How many of them would you say there were?"

"Hell if I know. To hear Cindy tell it, there were many of them. She always liked to play head trips on me. She was hot and she knew it. She was always throwing it in my face about how other guys were always hot after her. Hell, like I was lucky to have her or some damn narcissistic crap like that."

"Why do you use past tense, when referring to Miss Porter?"

"I did? Well, you know what I meant."

"I have no idea what you meant, Mr. Summers. All I know is what you stated."

"Hey now, I didn't make any damn statements!"

"You do not seem to have a very good opinion of Miss Porter, but by the same token, you say that nothing was awry between you two?"

Dale Summers lowered his eyelids over his deep-set dark chocolate brown eyes and gave Chad a steely glare. "Hey look, I don't like where you're trying to go with this line of questioning! You're trying to put words into my mouth."

"They're your own words, Mr. Summers. Where were you on the evening of Miss Porter's disappearance?"

"I was at my folks place. I went over there for dinner."

"You were there until what time?"

"I guess until 9:00 or about 9:30."

"So you're not sure what time you really left?"

Dale became increasingly agitated with the line of questioning. "How the hell was I supposed to know then, that I would need to know the exact time I left my own damn parent's house?"

"Where did you go after you left your parents' house?"

"I bought some beer and then went straight home."

"Where did you buy the beer?"

"I bought it at the convenience store."

"At which convenience store did you purchase your beer, Mr. Summers?"

Dale shifted his weight from one foot to the other and said, "Cindy's store."

"So you were at the store shortly before her disappearance?"

"I guess I was, so what? I didn't do a damn thing to Cindy. I could have her anytime I wanted her. Why in God's name would I want to hurt her?"

"I did not say that you did hurt her. Did you hurt Miss Porter, Mr. Summers?"

"Look, I'm going to get a damn attorney. You're trying to set me up."

"You're entitled to do as you please, Mr. Summers. May I suggest that you do not leave the State of Idaho for the time being? We may need you for further questioning. Have a nice day, Mr. Summers. I will see myself out."

"You do that and don't come back here again, unless you have a warrant."

Chad smiled at him and said, "Now that might be a good idea."

"Get the hell off my property, you dick wad!"

Chad wondered if the sheriff knew Dale Summers had been at the convenience store just before the girl disappeared.

Chad later decided that he would do some unconventional detective work. After all, what was a better place for it than a tiny town like this, where everyone knew everyone else's business or thought they did.

Next, Chad stopped at a local diner. The hostess offered to seat him at a booth, but Chad told her the counter would be fine. In fact, the counter was his goal. Chad picked the most populated part of the counter and sat down in the midst of some local good old boy types. But it was really the young waitresses whom he was the most keen on. The good old boys would help him lead the conversation in the direction which he wanted it to go, with perhaps just a little coaxing. The men at the counter eyed Chad up and down and fell silent in their casual back and forth banter.

One of the young waitresses behind the counter walked over, smiled warmly at Chad, and handed him a menu. "Would you like coffee, sir?"

Chad glanced at her name displayed on the pin upon her chest, "Yes that would be great, thank you, Karen."

She poured him a cup of coffee and sat a creamer down on the counter in front of him. "Just let me know when you're ready to order."

Chad studied the menu for a moment, and then he closed it and looked up. As if on cue, Karen stood in front of him with her order tablet out and her pen poised in the air above it. "I will have the Ranch Scramble."

"Would you like white, wheat or sourdough toast?"

"The sourdough toast, please."

"OK, it will be right up!" She smiled a little flirtatiously and turned away. Chad enjoyed watching the extra swing she applied to her butt cheeks for his benefit as she walked away.

And clearly, the old men up and down the counter enjoyed the show as well. A few chuckles came from some of the other men, and an old timer nudged the one sitting next to him and nodded in Karen's direction, just in case his counter mate had missed the show.

An old timer just could not help but to call out, "Hey Karen, it looks like you got your panties all in a bunch!" Laughter rang out all up and down the counter as Karen ignored the comment.

"You're not from around these parts are you?" the older man sitting to Chad's left asked. Chad knew that question would not take long to ask, and there it was, as if right out of a play book.

Chad turned slightly on the stool to face the older gentleman and said, "No sir, I am not."

"Just passing through?" his inquisitive counter mate asked.

"No, I'm here on business."

"What type of business?"

Chad could see the other older men at the counter were slightly leaning toward him, straining to hear. "I'm investigating the disappearance of Miss Porter."

"You're not one of our local boys. I thought they were handling the case?"

"They were, sir, and they still are."

"Well then, why did they send you here?"

The pretty waitress was back with the coffee pot. "Would you like a refill, sir?"

"Yes, thank you, Karen."

She filled his cup and paused for a moment, studying him intently with sultry blue eyes and asked, "You're with the FBI, aren't you?"

"That is correct," Chad replied. A silence fell all up and down the counter, but it was only temporary. Suddenly, everyone seemed to have questions all at once. Chad's job was to deflect as many of these questions he could. He was on a mission here to gather information, not to give it out.

"Did our local guys request help from the FBI?" the gentleman to the right of Chad asked.

"No, sir, they did not"

"Then, why are you here?"

"It is protocol. We're here to provide assistance to your local law enforcement."

"What happened that would make you guys come here? I know she got kidnapped, but don't our local cops take care of that? I'm Fred by the way." He held his hand out to Chad.

Chad shook the extended hand and said, "I'm Agent Chad Turner. And again, your local police are handling the kidnapping, but I'm not at liberty to disclose any details regarding the case."

Fred said, "Well the no good skirt chaser, whom Cindy was dating before she went missing, has already been in here sniffing up Karen's skirt. You would think he would have more respect for Cindy than that. Hell, she's only been gone for a few days. I sure as hell don't know what the matter is with kids these days."

The gentleman on the left said, "Fred, when you were younger, you would be doing the same damn thing, and you know it!"

"You're damn straight about that, Jim. But, at least I would have given it more than just a few days. It's clear to me that he didn't give a rat's ass about the poor girl."

Chad eyed Fred keenly and asked, "This is Dale Summers, whom you speak of?" Chad also noticed Karen seemed to suddenly become busier wiping down appliances, which set on the counter opposite to where the men sat. She had her back turned to them, but he knew she could hear every word being spoken.

Fred said, "Yes, it is Dale Summers, is he a suspect?" Chad noticed the question made Karen turn around, and now her full attention was focused on the men at the counter.

Chad took a long draw from his coffee cup and set it back down before he said, “Fred, at this point, anyone can be a suspect, until we rule them out.” Karen looked visibly relieved.

Jim said, “That whole dang family has been nothing but trouble in this town.”

Karen couldn’t hold her tongue any longer, “Not Dale! He hasn’t been any trouble.”

Jim quickly corrected her. “What do you call the time he got in trouble with the law for growing a pot plant?”

Karen had a quick comeback, “He grew it for his personal use.”

Jim was just as quick with his reply. “That is bullshit, Karen, and you know it. He is nothing but a drug dealer. He’s nothing but trouble. The apple doesn’t fall far from the tree. And look at the fact that he hasn’t even given Cindy two full days of respect before he is chasing you. He’s not going to treat you any differently, that you can be sure of.”

Karen looked around the restaurant as if she was looking for an escape route, but Chad was wrong about that, because instead she came out swinging. She was not done defending her man. “Jim, Cindy is not exactly the goody-little-miss-two-shoes, which everyone has her made out to be! She was sneaking around behind Dale’s back and trying to get back together with Cliff. She didn’t think Dale knew anything about it, but this is a small town.”

Chad remembered Cliff as one of her former boyfriends, but he was two boyfriends prior to the current one. Chad carefully posed his next question. “So Karen, if I have this right, Dale and Cindy were in the process of breaking up when she went missing?”

Karen said, “It’s not like that, Agent Turner. I know what you’re thinking. Dale wouldn’t hurt a fly. He just got tired of Cindy’s sneaky double talk. She is a tramp! Her family is some of the wealthiest people in this town. They own several businesses here, so everyone older thinks she’s a nice girl. Trust me, anyone who had to go to school with her knows differently.”

"Would you say she had enemies?" Chad asked.

"More than you have fingers," Karen shot back.

With his coffee forgotten, Chad leaned closer into the counter, and asked, "Who do you think were her enemies?"

"Oh, just about every girl Cindy stole a guy from. You know she would just do it for fun, just to see if she could. Some of them she would dump the very next day. She made fools out of them too, because she didn't want them at all, and she had the whole school laughing at them. That is, except, for the ones she had already pulled the stunt on before."

Fred spoke up this time and said, "Now, Karen, I wouldn't go talking bad about Cindy, if I were you. You never know when you might need another job in this town."

Karen's eyes narrowed to a slit; she pointed a finger at Fred and said, "See that is just it! Almost everyone in this town either works for her family, or has a family member who does, so almost everyone has to kiss Cindy's ass. Fred, I'm only telling the truth about her, which is something almost everyone else is afraid to do. Agent Turner, it would help your investigation if you could get the truth out of the people in this town."

Chad looked up and down the counter, and he wasn't sure they were cognitive that they were doing so, but almost everyone nodded their head in agreement with Karen. Chad knew then that this girl was on to something. It puzzled him why the sheriff seemed so blind to what seemed to be, at the moment, the true nature of this missing girl. Not having this kind of knowledge about the missing subject could certainly hamper an investigation. The kitchen rang a bell indicating an order was up, and Karen went to check to see if it was one of hers. She returned with Chad's Ranch Scramble and placed it on the counter in front of him. Chad said to her, "Thank you, Karen, and thank you for your honesty. You have been a great deal of help."

"Yeah, well they're right. If I ever lose this job, I will probably never work in this town again."

"You're a smart girl, Karen, and there is a great big world out there beyond these city limits. You will be just fine."

She smiled weakly at him and said, "I sure hope you're right, Agent Turner."

Chad finished his breakfast and paid his check. He gave everyone at the counter a casual wave and left the restaurant. Chad knew he would be going back there. Just that morning he had received a wealth of information, which would have taken him much longer to turn up.

Chapter 2

Once Chad got back in his car, he opened the folder that the sheriff had given him and studied it to get the address of Cliff Rodgers. He pulled up in front of a neat little house, with a white picket fence and an impeccably manicured lawn. Chad rang the doorbell, and an elderly lady answered the door. "May I help you, sir?" she asked.

Chad once again pulled out his badge and said, "I'm here to speak to a Mr. Cliff Rodgers."

"Oh dear, is it about the poor little Porter girl?"

"I'm not at liberty so say ma'am."

"Well, let me go see if my grandson is up yet. He works nights, you know."

"No, ma'am, I didn't know that." Chad wondered if Cliff worked the night the subject went missing. He was going to find out. Shortly, Chad saw a good looking young man walking up the hall, combing his thick brown hair back with his fingers. His grandmother toddled along behind him. Cliff squinted in the glare of the bright morning light. "Are you Cliff Rodgers?"

"I am, is there some kind of a problem? Did they find Cindy yet?" Chad could see what appeared to be genuine concern on the young man's face. Then, Chad realized that concern was curiously lacking when he had spoken earlier with Dale in regards to Cindy.

"I'm here to ask you a few questions about Cindy Porter."

"Yeah sure, I will be happy to help you with anything I can."

"Were you and Miss Porter seeing each other?"

"Well, not exactly."

"That does not answer my question, Mr. Rodgers."

"Well, what I meant to say is she wanted us to start dating again. Cindy said she realized that she made a mistake when she broke up with me, and she wanted us to get back together again."

"So you started seeing each other again?"

"No, it was not really like that. We just hung out once in a while and would talk for long periods of time. I didn't want to get back with Cindy in that way because it really hurt when she broke up with me. I'm sure you know what it feels like. I just didn't feel I could trust her."

"You thought Miss Porter was playing another one of her games?" Chad asked.

Cliff looked totally surprised, and asked Chad, "How did you know about that?"

"It is my job to know things, Mr. Rodgers. Was Miss Porter worried that anyone may be out to cause her harm in any way that you're aware of?"

"No, I can't think of anyone right off hand. There were a few guys who gave her the heebie-jeebies at the store where she worked." Chad thought, there it was again. Cindy was creeped out by a few male customers who came into the store. Cliff went on to say, "I guess they were probably harmless enough." Chad knew that sometimes a person's intuition tells them much. Hell, he used it almost daily in his own work. He would have his technicians comb over the video tape from the store to see who these regulars were and how many times a day they would come in. Chad would also be interested in even the frequent weekly customers. They could not discount anything in a case such as this one.

"Cliff, did Dale know Cindy was seeing you again?"

"Sir, this is a small town, and like I said, we were just hanging out a bit."

Chad said, "That can be misconstrued."

Cliff shrugged his shoulders and said, "Yeah, I reckon it could be."

"Do you think Dale Summers could be the violent type?"

"God, I hope not! Dale has a temper for sure, and a big mouth. He likes to talk tough but, other than that, I don't think so."

"We all have tempers, Cliff. However, some of us have just learned how to control our tempers better than others. Dale didn't give you any problems about the time you spent with Cindy?"

"No, the truth of the matter is, Dale was ready to move on, and she knew it."

"Did she suggest that to you in any way?"

"No, but then again she wouldn't. Cindy is the one who likes to dump people. I know that first hand. I'm very reluctant to be subjected to that again."

"I understand, so why did you entertain her?"

"I thought maybe we could just be friends. I still care about Cindy. I just couldn't trust her with my heart again. I still have a connection to her. I know a side of her many others don't see."

"And what is that connection, which you refer to, Cliff?"

"Underneath the confidence, which Cindy radiates to the world around her, she is really someone who is weak, unsure, and afraid."

"She is afraid of what, Cliff?"

"Cindy is afraid her charade will come crumbling down. Like a bird that is dying, it will act healthy right up until it falls from a tree, so its predators don't know it is weak."

"You really loved her, Cliff."

"I did, sir. I just couldn't trust her again. Being in a relationship with her is like being on a rollercoaster ride."

"Why do you say that, Cliff?"

"When we were dating, she would openly flirt with any other guy she chose to, right in front of me. Cindy didn't care how I felt about it. When I brought it up to her that it was hurtful, she would just laugh and call me silly. I knew I was going to be just another notch on her belt. I just didn't know when that was going to be."

"Did she flirt with other men right in front of you in this second go around, while she was trying to get back with you, Cliff?"

"You're an FBI agent, so you know a tiger can't change it stripes!"

"Humans are not animals, Cliff. They just act like animals sometimes. Did it make you angry, when Miss Porter flirted with other guys?"

"I said that it was hurtful."

"I heard you, but did it also make you angry? You two have a history together."

"Well, now that I give it some thought, sure it made me angry. How could it not. How would you feel in the same situation?"

"How I would feel is irrelevant to this case. I would like to make a request that you do not leave the state until farther notice. Thank you for your time."

Cliff's mouth fell open in astonishment, "I'm a suspect? I would never hurt Cindy! I loved her!"

"Have a good day, I will be in touch."

Cliff held the door open for Chad and, as soon as Chad stepped over the threshold, the door slammed hard behind him. Chad smiled and thought, yep, everyone has a temper. When he was seated behind the steering wheel of his car, he picked up the folder that the sheriff had given him and flipped it open. His eyes lingered momentarily upon the smiling, youthful face of Cindy Porter and then he scanned the list of known boyfriends. It was time to pay a visit to Tim Walker, who happened to be the boyfriend she had just before Dale Summers. Chad drove to the address listed in the folder. The neighborhood rapidly went from manicured lawns to shabby row houses, and then to even shabbier apartment buildings. It appeared Mr. Walker was not at the top of his game, whatever that may be at this point in his life. Chad knocked upon the door of apartment number four and got no response. He knocked again louder and there was still no response. He would have to pay Mr. Walker another visit. Chad turned to leave, when the door swung open. A skinny girl stood squinting with blood shot eyes into the morning sunlight. "Yeah, what do you want?" she asked with a hoarse voice.

Chad flashed his ID and said "I am looking for Tim Walker."

"Well, he isn't here."

"Where might I find him?"

"Hell if I know and I don't give a shit where he is!"

"How long has Mr. Walker been gone?"

"Two days. The bastard ran out on me without even saying a word."

Chad's interest peaked and he took out his note pad. "Can you tell me exactly when the last time you saw him was?"

"Are you deaf? I told you two days ago."

"I mean the exact time of day you last saw him."

"I saw him Thursday morning, when I left to go to work."

"The exact time please, Miss?"

"7:30."

"What is your name, please?"

"Jackie Banks."

"What do you know about Cindy Porter?"

"I know firsthand she is a game playing bitch."

"Why do you say that about Miss Porter?"

"I say that because, even after she dumped Tim, she would still flirt with him right in front of me. She just wanted to mess with his mind and piss me off. We had some big ass fights over that."

"You had fights with Miss Porter?"

"Hell no, but I should have smashed the bitch's smug face in. For all I know, Tim is with her right now. They have both been gone for the same amount of time. If you find them together, they will not need the FBI. They will need a coroner, when I get done with them."

"You have some pretty strong feelings about Miss Porter."

"Duh, you think, Einstein!"

"Are those fresh needle tracks on your arms, Miss Banks?"

Jackie immediately crossed her arms and said, "Get out, we're done here!"

"Have you ever considered harming Miss Porter and Mr. Walker?"

"If you find them together, hell yes, I will kill both of them!" she said. "Now, get out!"

"Thank you for your time, Miss Banks." Chad turned and left the apartment.

Jackie poked her head out the door and hollered after him, "When you find the bastard, you let me know." Chad ignored her and kept walking to his car. Chad knew the time had come to pay a visit to Cindy Porter's parent's home. Chad drove through town and then took the eastbound highway out into the country. The farms and ranches sprawled out on either side of the road. Cattle and horses grazed happily in their own little herds. Although some shared pastures, one species did not mingle with the other. Large herds of sheep, still with their heavy winter fleece, dotted the low rolling hills. Finally, he saw a driveway, which had huge stone pillars and was lined with tall trees for as far as he could see. A wrought iron sign, which read Porter Ranch, hung across the stone pillars. Chad swung his car onto the paved drive. Clearly, the wealth of this family far exceeded that of anyone else in this community, just as everyone had told him so far. The house was not a house at all, but a mansion sitting in the midst of formal gardens. A stable set a good distance away, where finely bred horses were being groomed and exercised.

Chad pulled his car up into the circular driveway in front of the mansion. As he approached the front entrance, water gushed and overflowed into triple tier fountains on either side of the walkway. Chad couldn't help but to think this place looked like something out of a movie set. He rang the doorbell and heard it chime on the other side. After just a few moments, a maid in the traditional uniform opened the door. He couldn't help but notice the iron creases on the uniform were impeccably crisp and straight. It reminded him of his early military experience, before he joined the special ops, but that no longer mattered then. All that mattered then was how he could complete a mission and come out of it alive.

"May I help you, sir?" the pretty maid asked. He smiled at her and flipped open his ID. "Oh, you're here regarding Cindy?"

"I am, Miss. Is Mr. or Mrs. Porter home?"

"Please come in, I will show you to the study." Chad stepped into the foyer of the home and was amazed at the grandeur of the stairway, which swept up into the upper reaches of the home. He had never been inside a house like this. "Please follow me," she said and smiled sweetly at him. Chad simply nodded and followed her. The dark cherry doors which led off the foyer gleamed with a rich luster. They were polished often, of that he was sure. The maid opened one such door and stepped through. She turned to him and said, "Please have a seat. May I get you something to drink?"

"No, thank you, I'm fine for now."

"As you wish, Mrs. Porter shall be down momentarily. I know she will be anxious to speak with you."

Within minutes, a middle aged lady burst into the room. Her face was strained, and her eyes were swollen and puffy from hours of crying. "Please, have you any news about my baby girl?" Tears seeped over the edges of her lower eyelids.

"I have been interviewing people who have been known to be close to your daughter all day, Mrs. Porter."

Chad was surprised when this well-groomed lady exploded, "What the hell are you talking about! The sheriff's office has already done that. All you're doing is wasting precious time. I want you to bring my baby back home to me! Sheriff Marker promised me your office could get us results and, damn it, that is exactly what I expect!"

"These things take time, Mrs. Porter."

Then she screeched at him, "We don't have time! My baby is out there somewhere. Don't you understand that! What the hell is the matter with you?"

"Please calm down, Mrs. Porter. I need to ask you some questions." Mrs. Porter looked at him incredulously and then collapsed into a nearby chair. Her shoulders shook violently as she sobbed into her hands.

The pretty young maid came into the room holding a glass of water and an open pill box, "Please excuse the intrusion but, Mrs. Porter, it is time for your medication," the maid said, extending the water and medicine out to Mrs. Porter.

Mrs. Porter lashed out with her right arm and knocked the water glass out of the maid's hand. It fell to the hardwood floor and shattered. "I refuse to be drugged anymore. I want my baby home, and I need a clear head to make damn sure it happens." The maid immediately stooped and started to pick up the broken glass. Mrs. Porter barked at her, "Leave us; you can clean the mess up later!"

"Yes, as you wish, Mrs. Porter," the maid said, promptly leaving the room and closing the study door behind her.

Chad tried speaking to the distressed woman again. "Mrs. Porter, I have already uncovered some new leads that the Sheriff's office may have overlooked."

The woman looked up at him with renewed hope on her face. "What new leads?"

"I am not at liberty to say."

"What the hell are you talking about? This is my daughter, you son-of-a- bitch," she yelled at the top of her lungs. Clearly, this woman was used to having people cater to her. She seemed to no longer respect others. "I want someone else on this case pronto. Not some inept, incompetent mealy- mouth, who will not tell me what the hell is going on!" She sprung up from out of her chair and said, "This stops here and now! I'm calling Sheriff Marker and getting your worthless ass replaced!" She stomped over to the phone, which set upon a nearby desk, and dialed Sheriff Marker's number from memory. "Hello, I need to talk to Sheriff Marker this minute, this is Dana Porter." Dana looked over at Chad and glared at him, while she waited for the sheriff to answer her call. "Hello, Sheriff, this is Dana Porter. I want another FBI agent on this case immediately! Why, because he will not tell me a damn thing that is what is going on. I have the right to know what is happening. I have the right to know everything that is going on. What? You have no idea how I feel. How dare you say that, Sheriff! It is not your child, who is out there somewhere, and you're sitting in your damn office, and this FBI agent is standing in my study!" She stopped talking for a moment and listened, and then looked over at Chad and said in disbelief, "What do you mean he's their top gun?" She listened for a few more minutes and finally nodded her head. Her face lost its color and she replied, "Yes, Sheriff, I understand," then she placed the receiver back in its cradle. She turned slowly, squarely facing Chad and said, "Sheriff Marker tells me the Agency has already assured him that you have an impeccable record, and that you are the Commander of the FBI's Special Tactics team. My Cindy is in trouble, isn't she?"

"We have not made that determination yet, Mrs. Porter. She appears to have been robbed and abducted. We will need a few of her personal items; preferably clothing which has been recently worn."

Mrs. Porter looked distressed when she said, "Our maid does the laundry daily."

"What about Cindy's bedding?"

Mrs. Porter looked relieved and walked over to the intercom mounted on the wall and, with a trembling hand, pushed a button. Soon, the young maid's voice said, "Yes, Mrs. Porter?"

"Amanda, would you please strip Cindy's bed, and bring me her sheets and pillow cases in plastic bags?"

"Yes, ma'am, right away, Mrs. Porter."

"Now, Mrs. Porter, may I ask you a few questions?" She sank back down into her chair and weakly shook her head in agreement. "Does your daughter have any known enemies, in the past or the present?"

Dana shook her head and said, "No, everyone loves my Cindy."

"Mrs. Porter, everyone has made enemies at some point in their life. Please try your best to remember. Your daughter is a very pretty girl; surely there were other girls who were jealous of her. Take your time and think back."

After a long pause, she looked up at him and shook her head. "Sure, there might have been girls who were jealous of her, but she was so nice to them, regardless of how they felt about her. She always eventually won them over."

"Your family has obvious means, so why did Cindy work the closing shift at Porter's Stop and Go?"

"My mother-in-law has always insisted that having family members working in our businesses is the way to build wealth for the family. She always said to keep it all in the family whenever you can, and I always thought she was right. I never dreamed something like this would ever happen. There are cameras everywhere in the store."

"They're very antiquated cameras. Images on the tape are very grainy. We will have our team of experts try to improve the quality. Rest assured they are using the best equipment available. Would your daughter have any reason to pull a disappearing act, like drug use, or addictions of any kind?"

"Heavens no, my Cindy is a good girl! She has always shown disdain for kids at her school who were into drugs."

"Mrs. Porter, Cindy's boyfriend, Dale Summers, got arrested for growing a marijuana plant."

"Well I'm sure Cindy didn't know anything about that. And, if she did, I'm sure she felt he could change. She always tried to bring the good out in people." Dana dabbed at her eyes with a wad of Kleenex crumpled up in her fist. "She is always so optimistic about the world around her." Her face scrunched up as a fresh wave of emotions washed over her body and she said, "You don't think they will hurt her do you?"

"I can only assure you this, Mrs. Porter; we will find her just as soon as we can. This case has the highest priority. Does anyone hold a life insurance policy on Cindy?"

Dana shook her head in affirmation and said, "Only her grandmother, but she has policies on all of her employees. It is just one of her standard business practices."

"I understand that there were a few of the regular customers whom Cindy had concerns about. Did she say anything about those individuals to you?"

"Only that a few of them gave her a case of creeps, but nothing which is really useful."

"I will decide what is useful, Mrs. Porter, that is my job here. Can you please expand on the previous question?

"Well, there was one in particular; he would buy a coffee and lurk around in the store. He always hung out at the counter and would try to make small talk with her. He would also chat up other customers. Cindy wanted to 86 him from the store, but her grandmother would not hear of it. He comes from an old local farming family here, and my mother-in-law has known his family for years. Cindy's grandmother did not want to make waves, because she thought he was harmless. Perhaps a little love sick, but otherwise harmless. Oh, my God, do you think she could have been wrong?"

"At this point in the investigation, anything is possible. Do you have a name and address where I might find this individual?"

"He is Todd Holmes, and he still lives on his family's farm in a little shack."

"Do you happen to know what age Mr. Holmes is?"

"He is much older than Cindy; that is what she found to be so creepy about him. He is in his late thirties."

"He works on his family's farm, I take it?"

"He does more of watching other's work, from what I've heard."

"People around here don't have a very high opinion of him?"

"He's lazy and looks unkempt. He is not exactly a chick magnet, if you know what I mean. It disgusts me that my mother-in-law would subject Cindy to the man gawking at her like that. And he loves his liquor; he has more than a few DUI's."

Soon, there came a gentle rap on the door of the study and Mrs. Porter said, "Yes, Amanda, come on in." Amanda entered the room and handed two small bags to Chad.

"Thank you, Amanda," Chad said to her.

She gave him a small curtsy and looked at Mrs. Porter, waiting to be excused. Mrs. Porter simply waved her away.

"Is there anything else which comes to mind, Mrs. Porter?"

Not that I can think of at the moment. My brain just feels like it is going to explode. I can't sleep. I just want my baby girl!"

"We will do everything in our power, Mrs. Porter, of that you can rest assured." Chad took a business card from the breast pocket of his blazer and handed it to her. "Here, take this; just in case you think of anything else which you think may be important, please call me on my cell."

"Please find my baby, Agent Turner."

Chad nodded and said, "I will see myself out."

Chapter 3

Chad left Dana Porter's estate and returned to town. He checked into Porter's Inn, where Chad's Agency had made reservations for him. A young male clerk stood alone at the front desk. Chad walked up to the desk and sat his bags down on the floor. The clerk looked up from his paperwork and smiled at Chad, "How may I help you, sir?"

Chad looked at the name plate upon the young gentleman's lapel and said, "I'm Chad Turner, I have been told that reservations have been made for me, George?"

George studied his guest registry for a brief moment and said, "Yes, of course, Mr. Turner, I have you right here."

Chad took this opportunity, since George didn't appear to be busy, to do some more work. Chad said casually, "George, I couldn't help but notice just about every other business in this town bares the Porter name. That is pretty impressive."

"Yes, it is impressive, especially if you knew the history behind how Mrs. Porter Sr. got her start. She practically built an empire on her own."

Chad put on his warmest manufactured smile and nonchalantly said, "Is that so?" It appeared that the clerk was bored and more than eager to have someone to talk to.

George replied, "When she first came to this country, she started out by selling goats on the street corners. People laughed at her at first and called her the little crazy goat lady. That is, until she started educating them about the many things which goats are good for. The local people around here started using them for milk because they were much easier to keep than a cow. And way back then, this town would even allow people to keep goats in their yards. Like it is now, most people around here were just poor working folks. So, she didn't stop there, she went on to teach them how to make cheese from the milk, and folks also got the added benefit that goats kept weeds and grass in the yards down. They were not used to eating goats but that also soon changed, when folks learned they could feed their family's better for much less. Her business exploded, and she began buying up houses here in town, one by one, as she could afford them. They were just little run down places at first. Then, she would turn around and rent them for whatever she could get. Again, people laughed at her and called her a slumlord, but I guess now she has had the last laugh. Many of the family members of the same people who were laughing at her, either work for her, or rent from her, or shop in her stores."

Chad said, "Wow that is quite an impressive story."

George nodded in agreement, smiled and said, "The good old days, huh?" George paused for a moment before he said, "But, as it goes, with that much success, trouble always invariably seems to follow."

"You're referring to the abduction of Cindy, George?"

"Well, there is that but, during these last few years, several of her businesses have been hit with arson also. She says her competition is trying to burn her out. But, no worries, we're very safe here, because Sheriff Marker has stepped up patrols of all Mrs. Porter's businesses."

Chad leaned forward and posed his next question, "George, did you know her granddaughter, Cindy Porter?" Chad saw George's demeanor instantly change. George's whole body stiffened, his brows furrowed, and a tic started on the left side of his face.

George cleared his throat, and said, "Yes, sir, everyone knew Cindy."

"Did you date Cindy Porter?"

"No, you couldn't really call it dating. She is out of my league, sir."

"So you did date her?"

"I had the misfortune of being one of her many boyfriends for a day, sir. I was her boyfriend just long enough to cause a split between me and the girl who, really cared for me. Cindy broke Tammy and me up. All Cindy really wanted was to make a fool out of me. That is how she got her kicks." George leaned forward anxiously and said, "Mr. Turner, this will be confidential, won't it? I really do need this job."

"Rest assured, George, anything I put into a report is for my agency's eyes only. What do you feel for Cindy now?"

George shrugged his shoulders and said, "Pity, I feel sorry for her. I see her for what she really is."

"And what is that, George?"

"An attention seeking whore, who just can't help herself; I don't think she will ever be happy."

"That's some pretty strong language, George."

"I'm telling you the truth, Mr. Turner. And, if this ever gets out, I'm done in this town. Do you understand me?"

"I understand, George, you have nothing to fear. I appreciate your honesty."

George slid a card key across the counter to Chad and said, "You will be staying in room 219. It is just upstairs and on the left. Would you like me to show you to your room, sir?"

Chad picked up the card key and then his bags and said, "No thank you, George, you have already been most helpful."

George flashed Chad a strained smile and said, "Just let me know if there is anything in your room which you find lacking."

"I'm sure my room will be fine. As long as there is a bed and pillow, I'm good; it has been a long day." Chad then turned and headed upstairs. He opened the door to his room and the bed was indeed a welcome sight. In general, his room was very nice for a hotel in such a small town. He unpacked his belongings and then hit the shower, even though all he really wanted to do was hit the bed.

He did some of his best thinking in the shower and, on a hard case, this was his routine. He brought the water up to temperature, stripped down, and stepped into a steaming shower. As hot water rippled over his toned, muscular body, he thought about the day's events and tried to piece together the puzzle. He still could not understand why Sheriff Marker had such a high opinion of the missing subject. Chad thought perhaps Sheriff Marker got the same information that Chad did and simply filtered it out. But, in law enforcement, a filter block gets in the way of an investigation. This subject had committed no legal crime, but Cindy Porter committed crimes of the heart over and over, and her victims were stacking up.

No one could take the robbery of Porter's Stop and Go at face value, especially since this girl got abducted. Chad could not shake a feeling that the money was never the motive to start with. Convenience stores were robbed all across the nation every day and, sometimes, clerks were killed but they're rarely abducted. As Chad thought about it, the more he felt certain that money was not the motive. The only scenario that he could come up with, if the money was the motive, was that this subject knew her robbers, and they took Cindy Porter to silence her. Chad turned off the water, dried off, brushed his teeth, hit the sheets, and went out like a light.

The next morning, Chad's alarm on his phone rudely interrupted a very pleasant dream. It took him a few moments to orientate himself to his unfamiliar surroundings. Then, he threw back his covers, put on a pair of sweats and went on a run. At six a.m., an occasional car would drive past him. The tiny little town was just waking up. Occasionally, a passing motorist would give him a friendly wave. Chad smiled and thought that is the charm of living in a rural town such as this one. For most folks here, being friendly to one another was just a way of life, but he knew for others it was a dog-eat-dog world, just like everywhere else. He could not help being jaded, because of his special ops training in his military career, and being a seasoned agent on the Tactics Team just changed one's view of the world in which they lived.

He returned to Porter's Inn, before heading back out to the little restaurant where Karen worked. Just as the previous day, she was there behind the counter. However, this day was different, Karen was not happy to see him this time. There was no friendly or flirtatious smile upon her lips, when she caught sight of him coming through the door. When he headed to the counter and sat down in the midst of local customers, she frowned. He smiled warmly at her and said very cheerfully, "Good morning, Karen."

She looked downright irritated now and replied in a dry tone of voice, "Would you like coffee?"

"As a matter of fact, I would," Chad said, as he reached for a menu which was tucked amongst condiments on the counter in front of him. Chad was happy to see that, at this hour, it was a different group of locals. They were much younger than the group yesterday. These guys looked like they were there to catch a quick bite before heading off to work. Yesterday's group was the late morning coffee drinkers, most probably retired.

Karen brought his coffee over and set it down in front of him. Some of it sloshed from Chad's cup onto the counter. Chad could see Karen didn't give a damn. He made his selection from the menu and gave her his order. Chad pulled a napkin from a holder and wiped up the spill.

He looked up and down the counter. He could not help but notice the conversation had fallen off considerably, since he had stepped through the doors into this restaurant. He knew everyone there already knew exactly who he was. Chad also knew why this group was not as eager to engage him as the group was yesterday. These men were probably all still working, or hoped to work, and therefore were beholden to the Porter family. Chad decided he would leave them be but, when he had finished his breakfast, he said to Karen, "I need to know what time you get off work and where you live. I have a few questions for you."

Karen openly glared at him but said, "I live at 210 Oak Street in apartment 6, and I will be home by 2:30 this afternoon."

"I will see you then."

"I'm looking forward to it," Karen said sarcastically. Chad ignored her comment, paid for his breakfast, and left.

When Chad returned to his car, he called his team members whom were working with Washington State police on the triangulation of Cindy's last call. "What have you turned up so far, Bruce?" Chad asked of Bruce Whipply, who was the best at triangulation of cell tower data which the agency had.

Bruce replied, "I've got it narrowed down to a one mile radius, Chad."

"That is fantastic, Bruce. Once again, my man, you have come through. I'm calling Dan right now to authorize two scent hound teams. I hope to have them on site first thing in the morning, if I can."

Bruce replied, "That cheap SOB is going to love that kind of turnaround."

Chad smiled and said into his phone, "He is just going to have to live with it, Bruce. Dan will just have to put on his big boy pants and pony up the bucks. Time is of essence here, and with your great work, we're getting this thing rolling much sooner than we had hoped."

Bruce replied, "Well then, I will see you tomorrow morning, but tomorrow afternoon I will be heading out, since my work here will be done by then."

Chad said, "OK, buddy, I'll see you then, goodbye."

"OK, I'll see you tomorrow," Bruce said, and disconnected his call with Chad.

Chad called Dan next. Dan picked up on the second ring. "This is Adams speaking."

"Hey Dan, this is Turner."

"I wasn't expecting to hear from you so damn soon, Turner."

"Well, this is your lucky day then, Dan. You need to authorize two scent hound teams ASAP. I need them on site in Washington State first thing in the morning."

"Why the hell do you need that kind of turnaround, Turner?"

"We got lucky on our triangulation, Dan; we had Bruce Whipply on it. And as you're well aware, this case has top priority with our agency."

"All of your cases have top priority, Turner."

"I don't call the shots, Dan."

"It sure as hell sounds like you're doing a damn good job of it to me, Turner. You just couldn't live with one hound team?"

"I said two scent hound teams, Dan. We have no time to waste here. My team on the ground in Washington State will let you know of the exact logistics; they will be calling you momentarily. I will be talking to you later."

"Of that, I'm sure; goodbye, Turner," Dan replied, and disconnected the call.

Chad spent the rest of the morning talking with his team in Washington State and making sure they had everything in place they needed from Dan. When Chad was happy that it was an all- systems-go, he took a break for a late lunch at a little fast food joint there in town. Shortly, it was time to go pay a visit to Karen. He found her apartment and knocked upon the door at exactly 2:30 pm.

Karen did not bother to question who was on the other side of the door, before she swung it open and motioned for him to come inside. "A young lady should never open her door without knowing who is on the other side."

"I knew it was you."

"And how did you know it was me, other than the time?"

"Because you're anal, I can spot an asshole a mile away."

"You were pretty friendly to me when you first met me, Karen."

"That was before you opened your mouth."

Chad smiled, and asked her, "Are you always so blunt, Karen?"

She smirked at him and said, "I'm just an honest woman, Agent Turner. Do you have a law against it?"

"No. Listen, Karen, while you're being so honest, I would like to ask you a few questions?"

"I'm all ears."

"Can you shed some light on why Sheriff Marker has a much higher opinion of Cindy Porter than the younger set of folks in this town?"

"Well, that should be an easy one for someone in your line of work."

"That is not a helpful answer, Karen."

"It is a no brainer, really, follow the money."

"You're saying Sheriff Marker is on the take?"

"It is common knowledge around here that Cindy's grandmother, old Mrs. Porter, has bankrolled every single campaign Sheriff Marker has ever run. And as far as him being on the take, I have no idea, but isn't it your job to find out? All I know is, anyone who gives old Mrs. Porter any grief, always winds up on the short end of the stick, if you know what I mean. For years now, I've had my customers who own businesses in this town tell me they can hardly get any patrol coverage, because the sheriff's deputies are busy patrolling the Porter businesses and property. And as far as Sheriff Marker's high opinion of Cindy goes, anybody would be a fool to bad mouth the slut in front of the sheriff. Everybody in this town knows he is old Mrs. Porter's butt boy, so to speak."

"Wow, you really like that family, Karen!"

"You wanted the truth, didn't you? I refuse to live my life in fear of that family, and their influence on almost everyone else in this town. The rest of them are all cowards as far as I'm concerned."

"Karen, what do you know about Todd Holmes?"

"Todd Holmes is a drunken scumbag."

"Do you think he would be capable of harming anyone?"

"Todd is capable of anything, if he thought he could get away with it. His folks are good people. They should have thrown him off their farm a long time ago."

"I've heard he has a fancy for younger women?"

"Yeah, he has tried to hit on me. He hung out at the restaurant for months. He would sit at the counter and drink coffee for hours and bullshit with the other customers. But the creepiest part was he would just sit there and watch my every move." Chad noticed that her body did an involuntary shiver when she said the latter.

"What can you tell me about Tim Walker?"

"Tim is OK. He used to have a real bad drinking problem, but he cleaned up. He keeps pretty much to himself, and I guess he always has."

"What about Cliff Rodgers, Karen?"

"Cliff is a real sweetheart. He took it really hard when Cindy broke up with him." Karen did a little sarcastic laugh and continued, "He really thought he could have a chance with Cindy. He was a fool."

"Well Karen, I appreciate your straight forwardness and your time you have given me. I will be in touch."

Karen held the door open for him and said, "You should be out there seeing if you can get anyone else in this town to talk to you."

"I'm working on it, Karen. Goodbye."

Chapter 4

The next morning, Chad pulled his car off highway 9 onto the shoulder. He was just about 12 miles outside of the little town of Elk in Washington State. Various vehicles lined the shoulder of the road on both sides. Chad could see that the handlers of the two scent hounds stood beside their dogs talking to a state trooper. Chad reached over and took the two plastic bags, which contained Cindy's pillowcases and sheets, off the passenger seat. He got out of his car and approached the men with the dogs.

The dog handlers stopped talking to the trooper and looked at Chad as he approached them. "Good morning, I'm Agent Chad Turner and here are the missing subject's personal items," Chad said, as he handed each one of the handlers a bag.

One of the handlers extended a hand to Chad and said, "I'm Sam Duncan, and I'm pleased to meet you, Agent Turner."

Chad said, "I'm pleased to meet you, Sam."

The other man extended his hand and said, "Joe Warren here, sir."

Chad shook Joe's hand and said, "Pleased to meet you, Joe."

"Likewise, I'm pleased to meet you, Agent Turner, and thank you for having us out."

Chad replied, "I'm very happy that both of you guys were able to be here on the ground with such short notice." Chad then turned his attention to the tall state trooper and extended his hand.

The trooper shook his hand and said, "Gary Reed, sir. My department will be happy to assist you in any way we can with your investigation."

"I appreciate it, Trooper Reed, let's all get started, shall we?"

Sam Duncan kneeled down in front of his hound and unzipped the plastic bag underneath the dog's nose. The dog immediately put his nose to the ground and went to work. As the dog led Sam down the side of the road away from the others, Sam looked back over his shoulder and said, "I'll be in radio contact as soon as we pick something up."

Chad turned to the other handler and said, "Joe, I would like you to drive a mile up the road and track back in this direction."

"You've got it, sir," Joe said and loaded his dog back into his vehicle and drove off up the road.

Chad heard another car approaching and turned around to see Bruce Whipply pull his car up behind Chad's car. Chad smiled and walked over to greet his friend. Chad looked at his wristwatch and said to Bruce, the moment Bruce stepped from his car, "You're late, Bruce!"

Bruce smiled and said, "Don't give me any shit, Chad, it is just too damn early in the morning for this stuff." Bruce opened the trunk of his car, took out his laptop, placed it on the hood of his car, and opened it. I sent you an updated file of the mapping of the triangulation. I was able to home in on the most likely locations, give or take a half of a mile or more."

Chad stepped up beside Bruce and studied the map on Bruce's laptop. Chad pointed at the screen and said, "Damn, Bruce, look at that!"

"Look at what?" Bruce asked Chad.

"Hot damn, there are only five roads leading off this one. And most of those just look to be service roads," Chad said, and smiled at Bruce adding, "Do you know what this means, Bruce?" as he happily clapped Bruce upon the back.

"No, I don't know what it means, but I'm sure you're going to tell me."

"What it means, my old friend, is we can possibly have this phase of the search wrapped up before the day is out."

Bruce pointed at the screen of his laptop and said, "We have already confirmed these two roads here lead to farmhouses."

Chad said, "The scent hounds will have to rule them in or out. She could be held at one of those. If that is the case, we will have to call Dan for the SWAT team."

Bruce said, "That last cell call from her phone could be an incredible stroke of good luck for us and the subject, if she is still alive."

Chad's cell rang just then and Chad took the call, "Turner here."

"Agent Turner, this is Joe Warren. My dog has a hit."

Chad smiled at Bruce and said, "That is fantastic information. What is your location?"

"I'm right at the head of the service road near the 23 mile marker."

"Excellent, stay right there, I'm on my way. I want to walk that with you."

"I'll be waiting right here, sir," Joe said.

Chad closed his phone, slipped it back into his pocket and reached his hand out to Bruce. "Hey, buddy, until next time, and thank you once again for a job well done."

"It's just another day for me, Chad. I hope you find the young lady, whichever way it turns out. It could possibly save the lives of many more. If these cases are connected, whoever is involved isn't going to stop, until we stop them." Bruce shook Chad's hand and watched him get into his car and drive towards the 23 mile marker.

Joe stood with his bloodhound by his side. Chad could see the dog was clearly excited, which was a damn welcoming sight to Chad.

Chad stepped out of his car and said, "Joe, that dog of yours is raring to go!"

"He is a young dog, but he is already showing a hell of a lot of promise. He comes from some good lines."

"Well, if all these cases turn out to be connected and the two of you help us crack this thing wide open, he's made a name for both of you." Chad and Joe set out following the young hounds lead, as the other vehicles pulled up on the side of the highway along with the other hound to help in the search. About a third of a mile down the service road, the hound veered off onto a rutted narrow track. The vegetation had clearly been laid flat by the wheels of a vehicle just recently. Joe glanced over at Chad. Chad smiled and gave Joe an encouraging nod. Both the men were excited. They continued to lead the search party down the road. The young hound pulled on his leash in his eagerness and wagged his tail as he worked the scent. The track went back from the service road for quite a distance, until finally they came upon a clearing in the woods. What Joe and Chad saw there in the middle of the clearing was a pair of denim jeans. Chad held his arm up in the air. It was a signal for them all to stop in their tracks.

Chad took his cell out of his pocket and called Dan. "This is Adams speaking."

"Dan, this is Turner, how soon can you have a crime unit out here?"

"I can have one to you tomorrow at sunrise, Turner."

"Dan, I'm talking today."

"Son-of-a-bitch, Turner, is there nothing I can do to please you and your prima donna attitude?"

"Dan, young women are disappearing, and while I understand this may come as a surprise to you, time is crucial in cases like this."

"I'll get on the horn and see what I can turn out today."

"Thank you, Dan. Your cooperation, as always, is appreciated. Also, I'll need a grid search team."

Dan rolled his eyes and said, "Tomorrow morning."

"It is always a pleasure working with you, Dan."

"I wish I could say the same, Turner," Dan said and ended the call.

Turner and his team taped off the immediate area of interest. While the team waited for the crime unit, the hound teams continued to work the surrounding area, but when they could not locate another scent trail, Chad thanked the two men and dismissed them for the time being.

The crime unit arrived, and Chad introduced himself to the team, which he found out was led by the head investigator, Chester Simpson. Chad watched as they did a meticulous search starting on the perimeter of the taped off area. The crime unit photographer took pictures of the scene before anything was bagged and tagged as evidence.

Later, Chad walked over and squatted down next to Chester, who was currently kneeling on the ground and closely examining the tire tracks. "What do you have, Chester?"

Chester glanced over at Chad and said, "It looks like we have two sets of tire tracks here, both of which appear to be of about the same time period. We will locate the best place to get plaster castings of each of the two separate tracks."

Chad said, "That is good news. We already know one of the tracks is probably that of the missing subject's car, but the other track is the one we need to expedite."

"What type of vehicle did the subject drive?"

"It is a Ford Focus," Chad replied.

Chester pointed at one set of tire tracks on the ground before them and said, "Then this track was possibly made by the suspect's vehicle. Some kind of truck would be my first guess judging by the width of the track. Do you have a make on the suspect's vehicle?"

Chad shook his head and said, "No, we don't have anything yet. All we have is a grainy surveillance video. It is being analyzed by our lab as we speak. There were several vehicles on the tape, and if those jeans belong to the subject, this track will be a boon to our investigation. Could you please have your photographer send the picture of the jeans to my laptop? I'll need to go back and pay the subjects parents a visit tonight. I hope to God the suspects left us a gift on the jeans."

Chester gave Chad a knowing look and said, "If there is anything there, our lab will find it. They may already be in the data bank, if we're lucky. And I will have the pictures sent to you in the next thirty minutes. Do you think she is out here?"

"I have no way of knowing for sure. The scent hounds didn't pick up anything beyond this point but, if they bagged her, anything is possible. We will know tomorrow after the grid search."

Chad looked on as the crime unit located the best two sets of tire tracks and mixed the dental stone in a gallon sized Ziploc bag. Next, they painstakingly poured it just along the outside lips of the tracks to not damage the evidence. Chad's attention was pulled away when he heard one of the investigators say, "Hey, Chester, we have something over here."

Chester was already on his way over when Chad caught up to him. Together, the two men approached the young investigator, and Chester asked, "What did you find, Tom?"

"We've found a good foot impression," Tom said, as he held his lighting source obliquely to the ground. And sure enough, almost like magic, a foot impression appeared where before there appeared to be none. Chad was amazed, as he always was, by the skill of a good forensic team working together.

Chester clapped Tom on the back and said, "That's a job well done, young man, we'll get a cast of it."

Chad said to Chester, "With your great team, all in all, we have had a very productive day so far. Now, I'm going to head back over the state line to pay the subjects folks a visit. Give me a call if you folks turn up anything else."

Chester replied, "I will be sure to do that." Alone, Chad walked back up the service road to the highway where he had left his car. The walk helped him to clear his head. He was not looking forward to another encounter with Dana Porter. But at least this time, if the jeans did, in fact, belong to Cindy Porter, he was bringing her a token offering of progress. He was seasoned enough to know this was never the type of progress that a family wanted to see, but he also knew that, until there was a body, there was still hope. He could never think of a gentle way to point this out to distressed loved ones. Chad put his car into gear, pulled out onto the scenic highway and thought about the day's events, as the miles slipped away underneath the wheels of his car.

Chapter 5

Soon, Chad was entering the city limit of Weaverville, which he thought would have been more appropriately named Porterville. The little town was already starting to roll up its sidewalks, and it was only 5:30 in the afternoon. He smiled and thanked God that he never had to grow up in a little town like this one, because the truth of the matter was, so few people who did grow up in small towns such as this one rarely left, and when they did leave, it was usually to join the military, which was often times their only way out.

People often leave the cities to retire in towns such as this one, only to die shortly after, of boredom he was sure. He knew his life was not for most people, especially those with roots. But he was bound to no one. He loved the travel and thrived on the excitement of the job. No day was ever the same. He never knew what to expect the next day or even if there was going to be a next day for him. He also knew people who did his line of work long enough often did not have to worry about retirement. He often wondered if retirement was even a goal of his. He was old enough now that he no longer felt invincible, but still he continued, because he loved this shit. Many guys sit on their sofas and watch this stuff on television, but not Chad Turner. He lived it.

Chad drove through the town and emerged out on the other side, where the green pastures carpeted the low rolling hills and fat bovines lie in the fading sunlight chewing their cud, unbeknownst of the impending slaughter. He dreaded having to show the picture of the jeans to Mrs. Porter. His past experience told him there was a ninety-nine percent chance that they did indeed belong to the missing girl. Expensive new jeans don't just get cast aside in the middle of nowhere. Soon, Chad saw the tall stone pillars, which stood on either side of the Porter's drive like sentries standing guard. Chad turned off the highway and took the long tree lined drive. As he drove past the stables, he could see the stable hands were busily feeding the horses their hay and grain and shoveling new bedding into their stalls. As he pulled into the circular driveway, he could see the fountains were flooded with soft up lights in preparation of the growing darkness. Chad walked up the path between the two fountains and rang the doorbell. Amanda opened the door and smiled brightly and prettily at him. The black and white traditional uniform she wore did nothing to hide her beauty. Chad said, "Hello, Amanda, is Mr. or Mrs. Porter in?"

"Yes, Mrs. Porter is home. Won't you please come in?" Chad stepped into the foyer. "Please follow me to the study. You will be more comfortable in there." Chad followed Amanda down the hall, while admiring the curves of her buttocks as she swayed them not so subtly in front of him. He toyed with the idea of mixing business with pleasure, but he knew it could be a real career breaker. He had seen older colleagues use poor judgment and get involved with much younger temptresses, whose only aim was to throw investigations. The men's behavior was always a career limiting move. Chad saw men, who were once rising stars in the force, be passed over for hot assignments time and time again. Many of the same men currently worked under Chad, and he knew what their limitations were.

Once they were inside the study, Amanda motioned to an overstuffed chair and said sweetly, "Please have a seat, Agent Turner. I will go summon Mrs. Porter for you." Chad could not help but notice her departing glace swept the whole length of his body. The young lady was definitely in the mood to frolic. Damn, Chad thought, he would have loved to have met her under different circumstances. Soon Chad was rudely jerked away from his pleasant fantasies of Amanda when Mrs. Porter entered the study and closed the door behind her.

"I hope you have brought me some good news, Agent Turner? God knows, I could use some."

Chad opened his laptop, which sat upon a coffee table before him, and said, "Mrs. Porter, we have located an article of clothing which we're hoping you can identify as belonging to Cindy."

Mrs. Porter walked over and sank heavily into a chair next to Chad. Chad pulled up the image of the jeans on his screen and slid it over closer to Mrs. Porter for her to view. Immediately, Mrs. Porter's face scrunched up, and she burst into tears. She doubled over in her chair and cupped her hands over her face and wailed into her palms and rocked back and forth. Chad knew the jeans were, in fact, Cindy's. He got up from his chair and walked over and laid a comforting hand upon Mrs. Porter's shoulder. She looked up at him with eyes filled with terror. "She's still alive? Please tell me she is still alive." Chad gently rubbed her shoulder, and she shrank away from his touch and sprang to her feet with lighting speed and surprising agility, and screeched into his face. "Tell me that she is still alive, damn it!"

Chad took a cautionary step back away from the distressed woman and said, "Mrs. Porter, all I can tell you is we're proceeding with that assumption."

"Where did you find them?"

"You mean the jeans?"

"Of course, I mean the jeans, you moron, where the hell did you find them?" She was screeching at him again.

"I can't disclose that information to anyone at this point in the investigation." Chad was anticipating her next move. She clenched her teeth like a mad woman and lunged at him. He jumped back and flashed his badge at her. To his relief, it worked. She stopped in her tracks and sank back down into the nearest chair and was overcome with her raw emotions. Just then, the door to the study opened, and a well-groomed man in his late forties stepped into the room. When he saw Dana crumpled in the chair wailing, his face immediately turned ashen, and his eyes started to glaze over with tears. Chad realized this was none other than Mr. Porter, the girl's father, and he had assumed the very worst. Chad immediately crossed the room and introduced himself. "Mr. Porter, I'm Agent Turner. Your wife has just identified an article of clothing which belongs to Cindy."

Relief instantly washed over the older man's face. "My girl is still alive?" he said, with hope resonating in his voice.

Chad nodded and said, "That assumption is the current focus of our investigation, Mr. Porter."

"What was the item you found?"

"The item was a pair of jeans."

"Where did you locate them?"

Dana said through her sobs, "The bastard will not tell us!"

Mr. Porter walked over to Dana, knelled down next to her chair, slipped his arms around his wife's shoulders, and pulled her up against his big barrel chest. "Dana, this gentleman has protocol he has to adhere to."

Chad said, "I can tell you we've been able to uncover more evidence that will be extremely helpful as this investigation moves forward."

Mr. Porter watched Chad's face closely as he said, "There is still hope that she is alive?"

Chad knew the older gentleman was asking for reassurance and Chad responded, "Sir, there is always hope. The agency is doing everything in its power to bring your daughter home as expeditiously as is possible."

Mr. Porter said in a strained voice, "Dana has reassured me that you're considered one of the FBI's top guns. We know we're blessed to have you on our case, but it is just so damn hard to feel blessed at a time like this one." Then he buried his face into his wife's hair, and they huddled together and wept.

Chad picked up his laptop off the coffee table and said, "I will personally be in contact with you at the first word of any new findings, Mr. and Mrs. Porter. I will see myself out."

Chad stepped out into the hallway and gently closed the door behind him, and when he turned toward the foyer he saw Amanda standing there. As he approached her she smiled, and he could not help to notice the smile, while pretty, had a predatory look about it. "I get off work in thirty minutes," she said suggestively.

"Well Amanda, I hope you have a pleasant evening."

"You could have a very pleasant evening. I really know how to relieve stress, and make a person forget all about it."

"I could sure use some of what you're offering, but I do not mix business with pleasure, sorry." Chad said, and reached for the door handle. Amanda slipped between him and the door, and thrust her chest up at him. He could see her pert nipples straining against the black cotton of her uniform, and then he realized she had removed her bra in anticipation of this encounter. He was sure, if she had not waylaid him here in the hallway, she would have stepped out of the garden when he was on his way to his car. Chad was relieved, when he heard the door to the study open. Amanda darted out of his way, and disappeared through a nearby doorway. Chad made his way out of the mansion and to his car. It was a hell of a long day, and the encounter with the hot-to- trot lovely maid had him feeling lonely between his thighs. In a city, or even a large town, he could have gone to any meat market and taken care of that feeling, but not in a tiny town such as this. And tomorrow was going to be yet another long and lonely day. He hated small towns.

Chapter 6

The following morning, when Chad pulled his car off highway 9 at the 23 mile marker, the road was already lined with cars and trucks of all different makes and models. It looked like they had a good turnout of people willing to do the grid search. Many of these folks were volunteers, who had worked on searches throughout the years for the sheriff's office. And Chad was aware the local folks on both sides of the state line were speculating that a serial killer was amongst them. The news of the disappearance of a beautiful, wealthy, young woman had traveled fast. Chad had just stepped out of his car when he saw the first van, with a tell-tale satellite dish on top, coming up the road towards them. "Fuck!" he said, as he slammed his car door shut. And behind that van was another. Chad walked up to a sheriff deputy and said, "What is this, a damn parade?"

"Yes sir, it looks like the vultures caught wind of this."

"You need to assign some guys to keep them the hell away from the search area."

"I will take care of it right now, sir," the young deputy said, and strutted toward a small group of other law enforcement officers, some of which were state troopers. Chad started up the service road toward the search area. When he arrived there, he saw the search coordinators where already instructing the searchers on how to carry out the search. It was going to be a tight grid search. They had a good turnout of willing and able bodied people, and Chad didn't want them to miss a thing. The morning mist was just lifting from the wooded area when, almost shoulder to shoulder, the searchers began.

Chad was just starting to relish a small sense of satisfaction, when he heard a voice behind him. "Excuse me, Agent Turner; I understand that you're leading this investigation for the Bureau?" Chad turned around and saw a gorgeous, tall redhead standing in front of him. She was holding a microphone in her hand, and a cameraman was standing just to the left of her. Chad could see by the flickering light on the camera that they were rolling.

Chad said, "We will hold a press conference in the near future, Miss, but until then, you and your crew are interfering with an investigation."

The redhead persisted, "Is this the work of a serial killer, Agent Turner? And how soon will it be before this and the surrounding communities can feel safe again?"

Chad motioned for one of the troopers to come over. When the trooper was standing in front of them, Chad said in a firm voice, "Make it plainly understood that anyone else from a news agency which crosses the line that has been established for them will be immediately arrested, and all their equipment will be confiscated by the Bureau!"

The woman was a shark, "Agent Turner, the good folks of this community have the right to know what is happening on their doorsteps!"

"Would you like to be the first example, Miss? It should take your station about six months to get all their equipment back, including the van." The redhead glared at Chad and let the trooper lead her and her cameraman back to where the other reporters were gathered behind a bright yellow tape. Chad's phone rang and he answered, "Agent Turner here."

"Turner, this is Chester. I have some good news for you!"

"Good news is always welcome, Chester, in my line of work. What do you have?"

"The tire casting we took shows the vehicle, which you're looking for, has a bad aliment problem. And the tires on it are old Firestones, with not much tread left."

"Well that's great news! That's just about one fourth of the vehicles on this side of the state line and the next."

"Oh, come on now, Turner, I was feeling good about this!"

"I'm sorry Chester. I just had a run in with a nasty reporter. It is like a carnival out here. There must be about fifty news vans out there on highway 9. Some women are just not compatible. I didn't mean to snap at you. Your information will be of considerable help, when we home in on the make and model of the vehicle. Are there any other deformities on the tires?"

"No, there were none that we were able to detect."

"OK buddy, thank you for the information. And I do appreciate it."

"Turner, there is one more thing."

"What is it, Chester?"

"The lab has detected traces of semen on the jeans."

"That is fantastic news, Chester, why the hell didn't you say so to start with?"

"I was saving the best for last."

"Hell yes, my man, I owe you a beer. You have just made my whole day! Has it been run through the data bank yet?"

"The team is in the process of running it as we speak!"

"Call me the second you know anything."

"I'll put you on speed dial. I'll talk to you later, Turner."

"Keep up the good work, Chester," Chad said, and ended the call. Chad's spirits were buoyed for the first time that day, because now it felt like the investigation was starting to hum along.

Chad saw a scuffle break out over where the reporters were corralled, and then an older man broke through the line and dashed toward Chad. A sheriff's deputy was in hot pursuit of the sprinter in front of him. The older man ran up and stopped in front of Chad and held up a poster of a beautiful brunette. The deputy started to grab the older man's arm, when Chad said, "Give him a moment to speak, deputy."

"This is my little girl! She has been gone for three years! I see all these people searching for this rich girl, and it is on the news all over the country. The news is saying the FBI's special tactics team has been deployed to find this rich girl. What about my baby daughter? She's still out there somewhere and nobody cares!" Tears started streaking down his face and he added, "Nobody gives a damn about her anymore. Her being gone has ripped my heart out!"

Chad cleared his throat before he replied to the anguished father, "Sir, we are launching this investigation because our goal is to bring your daughter home and many others just like her. We're working under the assumption that Cindy Porter's disappearance may be connected to your daughter's disappearance."

The man started sobbing and said, "I just want my baby back is all. I just want her to come back home." The deputy gently took the grieving father by the arm and led him away.

The morning wore on without further incident, until a deputy walked up to Chad and said, "Our office just received a call that two hikers have run across a burned out car, which was partially hidden from view by brush, which someone piled around it."

"Can someone from your office show me where the location is, and has the area been taped off?"

"A deputy is en route as we speak to do exactly that. I'm available to take you there. Do you want to ride along with me, or follow?"

"I will follow," Chad said and together the two men walked down the service road toward their cars. A late arriving reporter and cameraman tried to get information from them as they walked along the road, but it was to no avail. Once Chad was in his car, he called Dan, as he followed the deputy down the highway.

"This is Adams speaking."

"Dan this is Turner. I need your authorization for Chester's team to work another location for us."

Dan sighed and said, "I'll expedite it."

"Thank you," Chad said and ended the call. They drove through the scenic little town of Elk, and about twelve miles out of Elk they pulled off onto another service road. Chad followed until they reached a parked patrol car, which was blocking further access to the road. The other patrol car was vacated, however, and a rutted track led off to the left side of it. Together, Chad and the deputy walked up the track. Chad could see tire tracks, which recently had laid the wild grass and weeds flat. Soon the other deputy came into sight. He was standing next to a charred mound of brush. Chad could see this was not an attempt to hide the car at all, but was clearly an attempt to set a forest fire.

The deputy, who showed Chad the location, turned to Chad and asked, "Do you think she is in the car?"
Chad replied, "There is only one way to find out. Chester and his team should be here shortly." Chad stayed on the scene until Chester and his crew arrived.

Chester was all smiles, when he walked up to Chad and shook his hand. "Good to see you again so soon, Agent Turner."

"Chester, tell me why are you looking so damned happy?"

"Because, my guess is before the day is out, you're going to owe me two beers instead of just one."

"Just what makes you so damned sure about that?"

"I've had just a few more years at this than you, Turner. And when I see a failed attempt to burn down a forest, I get all giggly inside."

"You're a tree hugger, Chester? I would have never pegged you as the type."

"No, because, when someone thinks they're going to burn down a forest to cover a crime there is usually a treasure trove of evidence left behind, because they get sloppy and careless." Just then, Chester's cell phone rang, and he took it out of his pocket, checked the number, and answered the call, "Chester here. Yes, I'm here with him now, what do you have?" Chester looked at Chad, smiled and then said into the phone, "Good deal, Fred, bag it. Good, I'll talk to you later."

"What do you have, Chester?"

"It'll cost you a second beer!"

"OK, you've got a deal."

"They found a cell phone, which had no tracks around it. My teams guess is that it was chucked into the woods."

Chad said, "I hope there is a set of prints on it."

"If there are prints on it, my lab will find them. Excuse me, Chad; I've got to get my team started on this task at hand."

Chad smiled at Chester and motioned his arm in the direction of the large mound of brush, which had the burned car at its center, and said, "Please, be my guest." Chad looked on as Chester's forensic team took more castings of tire tracks and foot prints. This time they got four sets of foot prints. Chad deduced two of the prints would be from the hikers who had found the car.

Chester called out excitedly to Chad, "Your suspect just might be a smoker."

Chad walked over to where Chester was standing, and saw one of the forensic team members pick up a few cigarette butts off the ground with tweezers and place them in small evidence bags. Chester said, "It is my guess these do not belong to the hikers who found this, because they probably are tree huggers. What do all of your years of criminal profiling tell you about tree huggers, Chad?"

"All my years of criminal profiling has taught me that tree huggers generally are not smokers, especially while they're hiking in the woods."

Chester said, "We'll run DNA analysis on these, and maybe we will have a match with our trace of semen."

Chad replied, "Yeah, and then all we have to do is find out who the hell it belongs to."

"That is always the million dollar question," Chester said. Chad nodded and walked over to where other members of Chester's team were methodically removing brush from around the car. As he watched this painstakingly slow process, he tallied up the possible evidence in his mind. So far they had five shoe castings, two cigarette butts, a cell phone, jeans with semen, and a burned car, of which the contents, if any, where unknown at this time. Chad's cell phone rang, "Turner here."

It was one of the technicians from the Bureau's lab and he said, "The vehicle which seems to be the most suspect at the time of the robbery and abduction is an older two-tone Ford pickup with an extended cab. It is white over tan and looks to be a 1990 to 1994 model."

Chad asked, "Were you able to get a license plate number?"

"Negative, we could not even pick up a partial, because the plates were out of view."

"I hope you were able to enhance the images of the guys who abducted her?"

"We were, but since they were both wearing a ski mask, all we can tell is they're Caucasian and both have brown eyes."

"Is it good enough that we can release it in a bulletin?"

"I would say no, simply because you would waste a lot of time and resources on false hits. I would say the only way this would be helpful is if you had two guys to match it to. And even then, you would need a lot of other solid evidence to back it up."

"OK, send me what you have, and I'll take it from there. Thank you," Chad said. He ended the call to make another one. He called the department of motor vehicles at the Bureau. He asked them pull the address for every white over tan 1990-1994 Ford pickup within a hundred mile radius on both sides of the state line. He and his team would start with the closest ones, and if nothing panned out there, they would have to broaden their search. The type of tires Chester had identified from the castings could certainly belong to a vehicle such as this one. Chad felt like the pieces were slowly starting to fit together, one by one. By this time, the forensic team had uncovered enough of the car to tell it was, indeed, a blue Ford, although it took a trained eye to find any paint which wasn't charred off the car altogether. That was another piece which fit perfectly into place. A gas canister was recovered and was bagged as evidence, but Chad knew it was going to be of almost no value, because it had been engulfed by the flames. Chad walked around to the back of the charred vehicle and stood beside Chester. Together, they watched as two of the forensic investigators took crowbars and pried open the trunk. Chad realized that he was holding his breath, as the metal tools grated sharply against the metal of the blackened trunk. Burnt debris, mostly ash, floated off the backend of the car and drifted to the ground. And with one last screech of metal against metal the trunk popped open. The trunk held the remnants of a spare tire and jack. Other than that, the trunk was empty. Clad felt relief wash over his body. There was still possibly hope for the Porter girl, but time was running out. Chad felt adrenalin rush through his body. He and his team were going to push harder than ever to find this girl.

Chester looked at Chad and said, "It is always a relief to see an empty trunk."

"Yeah, it sure the hell is." I have a few house calls to make. I'll catch up with you later, buddy." "OK, Chad. I will let you know if anything else turns up."

Chad drove back to the grid search area. After confirming nothing else was found, he instructed them to call off the search of the area. If there were any prints on the cell phone found there, then it had been a very productive endeavor. The reporters swarmed all around him, shoving their microphones in his face, and all shouting questions over each other. He pushed his way through the crowd and made his way back to his car. He opened his laptop to confirm that he already had a list of addresses sent to him from the DMV records department. He was going to start on this side of the state line first. This side of the state line was the last known location of Cindy Porter's abductors, so it just made logical sense.

Chapter 7

Chad's first destination was a little country road right off highway 9. He turned off the highway onto a graveled lane, which ran past several dilapidated farm houses. His destination turned out to look no different from its surrounding neighbors, with the exception that it appeared to aspire to be a junkyard. He parked his car and noted two pit bulls lunging against their chains. The chains he was sure were in good working order, but the shoddy doghouses they were chained to were questionable. Before he approached the ramshackle house, he placed his right hand upon the butt of his Glock.

A short, potbellied, old man opened the front door and said, "What brings you to my yard, young fellow?"

Chad flipped open his badge case and said, "Sir, I'm here to inquire about your two tone Ford pickup."

The old man's face lit up and he said, "Oh, do you want to buy it?"

Chad said, "No, sir, I do not." Chad watched as the happy expression slipped from the old man's face.

"Well then, what is it that you want with the truck?"

"May I see the vehicle, sir?"

"Give me a moment to get my shoes on," he said, and walked away from the door. Chad changed his location on the porch to a more defensive one near an old washing machine. Soon the old man was back and said, "It is sitting in the backyard. I don't know what the hell it is that you want with the old thing. It has a broken axle, but the engine is a damn good one." Chad followed the man around the outside perimeter of the house to a much smaller junkyard in the back. And there among the rusting automobiles of various makes and models of different vintages sat the two-tone Ford pickup. It was obvious at the first glance this pickup had not been moved for months, if not years.

Chad said, "I'm sorry to have bothered you, sir. Thank you for your time."

"Do you mind telling me what it is you're looking for, and why?"

"I can't disclose any information, sir. Have a good day."

"Goddamn government, always snooping into everyone's business!" the man grumbled, on his way back into his house. Chad returned to his car and determined what his next stop was going to be. It was an address just outside of the next neighboring town, Bear Creek. Chad followed highway 9 toward the town of Bear Creek. Five miles before the city limits of Bear Creek, Chad turned off the highway onto a gravel road, which was badly pitted with potholes. The landscape was pretty much the same as the last gravel road he was on except, on this road, the dilapidated houses were much smaller and spaced closer together. He saw the address he was looking for, painted on a graying and warped square piece of plywood. He pulled onto a dirt driveway and stopped in front of a decaying house. Chad walked up to the front door and knocked, and immediately there was a chorus of barking dogs. From the sound coming from the other side of the door, there were big ones and little ones, and everything in between. He heard someone yell shrilly, "Shut your damn mouths!" The dogs ignored the command and continued on with their serenade.

The door creaked open just a crack, and an older lady with dyed orange hair, which was showing about two inches of grey at the roots, peeped out at him. "What the hell do you want?"

Chad opened his badge case for her and said, "I would like to have a word with you, Miss Newton."

Miss Newton frowned , opened the door a bit wider, and squeezed her sort, fat body outside, kicking a small dog, which had tried to escape the house back inside in the process. "What do you want with me?"

"Do you still own a two tone Ford pickup?"

"I do, why do you want to know? What the hell have my two boys done this time?"
"Are your two sons in possession of the pickup at this time?"

"Do you see it in the yard?"

Chad reached into a pocket and pulled out a note pad. What are the names and ages of your two sons, Miss Newton?"

"I'm not going to tell you a damn thing, until you tell me what you want with my two boys!"

"There has been an incident involving a two tone Ford pickup, Miss Newton, and we do not know if your two sons have been implicated in that in any way. My job with you here today is to rule your sons out."

Her demeanor softened immediately, and she grinned showing rows of broken and rotten teeth. "Well, why didn't you say so to start with? My boys are good boys. My oldest is Jeff, and he is real bright. I'm so proud of him. He almost graduated the eleventh grade, and he would have if that friend of his hadn't up and disappeared."

Chad's attention peaked, and he leaned a bit closer to the woman in front of him. "Your son was friends with Ellen Cutter?"

"Yes, did you know her?"

"No, ma'am, I did not. Please go on, I didn't mean to interrupt."

"Well, as I was saying, he was real close to finishing high school, when his friend Ellen disappeared. When she disappeared, he just went to moping around the house, and he began going off into the woods for days at a time and cutting school. I had no idea he was so close to her. You know boys; they never tell their mother anything. He was all depressed, I guess. Then, later on, my other boy Randy, my youngest, started cutting school too, and going off into the woods with his big brother. The truant officers came out for a while looking for them when they cut school, but pretty soon they gave up. They gave up too damn easily, if you ask me. The truant officers tried to threaten me, like I had something to do with it, right? I didn't know where they were. Hell, I didn't even know they were cutting school for the longest time. And those truant officer bastards tried to blame me. I wanted them to get their education too, but do you know how damn hard it is being a single mother of two almost grown boys?"

"I can only imagine how hard it must be for you, ma'am. Do you know where your sons are now?"

"I have no idea where they are."

"When is the last time you saw them?"

"It was two days ago."

Chad's interest intensified. "Can you give me an exact time?"

"It was about noon, they were gathering up some grub to take to their fort. They have had a fort in the woods for years now."

"Do you know the location of their fort?"

"Heavens no; they would never tell me! They call it their hideout. Boys only kind of thing, you know how it is."

"Do either one of your sons have a cell phone?"

"Jeff's got one, but he won't give me his damn new number, because he says I harass him all the time."

Chad handed her one of his business cards and said, "Would you please ask either one of your sons to call this number, when you see, or talk to them again? Thank you for your time, Miss Newton."

She took the card and said, "I certainly will."

Chad called Dan the moment he got back into his car.

Dan answered the call, "Adams speaking."

"Dan, this is Turner. I need you to have a tap put on the phone of Ginger Newton at 1467 Cider Lane here in Bear Creek, Washington. And I need an all-points bulletin put out for one Jeff Newton, and Randy Newton, both of the same address. They were last known to be driving a two tone Ford pickup registered to Ginger Newton. And I need you to get Bruce to do a triangulation of the last cell activity for either one of these men for me, and tell him to keep track of any cell phone activity, until we have them in custody. Also, I need to know if either one of them has a .40 caliber registered to them, or either one of their parents."

While Chad was still sitting in his car in Ginger Newton's driveway, she was dialing Jeff's cell phone. To her surprise, Jeff, who usually ignored most of her calls, answered on the first ring. "Yeah, what do you want, Ma?" He sounded more irritated than usual.

"What have the two of you gone and done this time, Jeffery?"

"What the hell are you talking about now, Ma?"

"That is what I'm asking you, Jeffery? What has your nitwit brother talked you into this time?"

"You need to start making some sense, Ma!" Jeff was starting to sound alarmed.

"Why is there a guy from the FBI sitting in a car in my front yard?"

Jeff said, "Son-of-a-bitch!" and he immediately ended the call.

Randy was driving the pickup, when Jeff had taken the call from their mother. He looked over at Jeff and saw Jeff's face grow red with anger. "What did she want?" Randy asked Jeff.

"Ma, and the rest of the fucking country, wants to know what we have been up to!"

"What are you talking about? How the hell would anybody know anything? You told me this was foolproof! You son-of-a-bitch, you promised me this would be foolproof and then you grabbed the damn girl. You bastard, it is your fucking fault we have the cops after us. If you hadn't taken her, none of this would be happening right now!"

Jeff doubled up his fist and delivered a blow to his kid brother's right cheek, and the pickup swerved on the highway. "I need to get rid of my phone right now," Jeff said.

Randy glared at his older brother and said, "If you sucker punch me again, I will kill you." Jeff ignored Randy's comment, rolled down his window and threw the phone out the window and over the embankment.

Randy gave Jeff an anguished look and asked, "What the hell are we going to do now, Jeff? We need to just let her go."

Jeff looked at Randy and shouted, "Are you out of your fucking ever-loving mind? Do you know what they will do to us, if they ever find the hideout?"

"But I didn't kill anyone, Jeff. If we just let her go, they will go easier on both of us."

"Well, little brother, I have a plan. Look, they don't have any proof that we've done anything. As long as neither one of us talks, it stays with us, until the day we die. Now first, we need to ditch this truck and get us a new ride. Let's go over there and check out that mall." Randy took the nearest off ramp and steered the pickup into the parking lot of the shopping center. They were cruising very slowly, until Jeff said, "That is perfect."

Randy asked, "What is perfect?" Jeff pointed at a little Honda Accord and smiled. Randy smiled back at his older brother and said, "Sweet!" Their dust-up back on the highway was long forgotten, as Randy worked as a lookout, while Jeff hotwired the car.

Jeff said to Randy, "You follow me in the pickup, and I will pull over when I find a good place to ditch it, and the Feds can cool their heels while they hunt for it." Randy nodded and followed his brother back onto the highway. They drove out of town for about six miles, until Jeff pulled off the highway and onto a road, which they both knew led to the river. After about a mile, Jeff pulled the Honda off to the side of the road, and Randy pulled the pickup up behind the car. Jeff got out of the car and walked to where Randy sat in the pickup.

Randy got out and said, "That's it, we're just going to leave it out here in plain sight?"

"No, you nitwit, we're going to roll it into the river!"

"You're going to roll mom's pickup into the river?"

Jeff replied, "We need to buy some time to just lie low. She has some insurance on it, maybe. We'll tell her later it ran out of gas, and when we came back it was gone."

"She'll never believe that shit!"

Jeff looked at Randy and rolled his eyes, "I don't really give a crap if she believes it or not! Now, how about some help from you?" Jeff said, getting into the truck. He backed it up, and drove it to the edge of the water and stepped out. Together, with one on each side of the vehicle, they rolled the truck down the bank, and into the water. The nose of the truck dipped under the surface of the water, and the truck just bobbed like that on the surface, like some strange type of buoy. Then with eerie gurgling sounds, it disappeared beneath the surface. Jeff smiled with immense satisfaction.

"Mom is going to be pissed!" Randy said.

Jeff said, "Come on, we need to go get some new plates for this car." Together, they got into the Honda and drove back out onto the highway in the direction of town. Soon, they pulled off onto a country lane about half of a mile up the road. They drove up the lane, until Jeff found what he was looking for, a small house that looked secluded from the others. It had several trucks sitting near an old barn. Jeff took the license plate off the Honda and snuck onto the property. He removed the plate off one of the vehicles and replaced it with the Honda's plate. As he approached the Honda, he waved the plate at Randy, "They will never notice it is missing."

Randy said, "They won't notice it missing until they get pulled over someday." Jeff quickly went to work putting the newly acquired plate on the back of the Honda, and then he drove the Honda within a mile of their hideout. Then, they hiked the rest of the way in over the thickly forested terrain.

The hideout had been built in the previous century, long before the first Ford was a reality. It set obscured from view of the river by overgrown brush, even though it was built just above the riverbank. For what Jeff wanted it for, it was perfect. The two brothers had discovered it quite by accident one long hot summer years prior, when they were setting out animal traps. At first, it was just a place to hang out when they cut school and to consume stolen liquor, but that did not last long. Jeff had made sure Randy was sworn to secrecy with a blood brother pact. Jeff knew the two were already blood brothers, and he got a kick out of how seriously the nitwit took it, when they had made small cuts on their hands and smeared their blood together.

Jeff unlocked the padlock on the ramshackle door and the sunlight cut into the darkness of the little cabin. When they stepped over the threshold, Randy closed the door and slid all the locks into place. The room would have been totally dark except for the slim cracks between the boards that covered the windows. On the inside, wire grates were bolted over the windows, so the boards could not be accessed from the inside. Jeff unscrewed the top off his most recent illegally acquired object of desire, and turned the bottle of dark rum up to his lips. The dark amber liquid burned pleasantly down his throat. He smiled and wiped the dribble off his chin and passed the bottle to Randy. Randy turned the bottle up and chugged it until Jeff snatched it back away from his brother. Jeff growled at Randy, "It's not beer, you moron!"

"I know what the hell it is! Give it back to me!"

Jeff took a long pull from the bottle and said, "Not if you're going to chug it like that."

"I was thirsty," Randy said. Jeff begrudgingly handed the bottle back to him. Randy nodded toward the only interior door in the shack and asked, "Are you going to give her something to eat?"

Jeff reached for the bottle and snatched it from Randy, "What do I care, if she eats, or not?"

"Jeff, it has been two days! The least you can do is let her have some water!"

Jeff took the keys out of his pocket and threw them at Randy, "Go suit yourself! Just don't get carried away with your sympathy party."

Randy opened a can of chili beans, got a bottle of water, and unlocked the padlocked door. Cindy sat upon the floor with her hands and feet bound by duct tape. She cowered deeper into the corner of the room, when she heard the door being unlocked. When Randy stepped into the room, her eyes were wide with fear. As Randy approached her, he said, "I've brought you something to eat." He smiled at her and held out his offering proudly. Randy kneeled down in front of Cindy and said, "Now, I'm going to take that tape off your mouth, so you can have some water and eat this. But if you start screaming for help, Jeff is going to get irritated and come in here, and he is going to knock the crap out of you like he did the last time you tried that stunt. You don't want it to happen again, do you?" Cindy vigorously shook her head no. Randy smiled again, because he was pleased that he had gotten through to her. To further drive his point home he added, "Besides, when we walked you in here, you saw for yourself there is nobody to hear you scream. There is nobody out here except for us and the critters."

He set his offerings down upon the roughly hewn plank flooring and ripped the tape off her face. She cried out in pain, because part of her skin came off with it. Her face was battered and swollen from the many blows from Jeff's fist. "Please help me?" she pleaded in a whisper. "My family is very wealthy, and they will reward you generously."

"You know what I would be rewarded with? I would be someone's butt boy for the rest of my life; that would be if I was lucky enough not to get the death penalty!"

"But they won't give you the death penalty for robbery and kidnapping."

"Look, you had just better shut up, or I'm going to put this tape back on your mouth, and you're not going to get anything to eat or drink!"

Tears slipped from Cindy's eyes and she nodded that she understood. Randy said, "That's a good girl." He held the water bottle up to her lips, and she drank thirstily. Next, he dug a plastic spoon into the chili beans and said cheerfully, "Open the hanger," while making little noises like an airplane.

Cindy knew neither of these brothers was dealing with a full deck between their ears, and that made them both even more dangerous. You can try to reason with a sane person, but an insane human was as unpredictable as a wild animal. Cindy tried to resort to one of the things that had always worked for her; she turned on her charm. She whispered in a husky voice, "You know, if I had met you sooner, you would not have had to resort to kidnapping me. You're one hell of a hot hunk! Jeff must be very jealous of you? Actually, it is one hell of a turn-on that you kidnapped me. It would be so great if it was just you and me living out here in these woods without a care in the world." She looked at him with the most seductive look she could muster up under the circumstances.

Randy grinned and set the can of beans down and said, "You really like me?" Cindy ran her tongue suggestively over her lips and batted her eyelashes at Randy. "Then, show me, baby!" He wrapped his arms around her and pulled her toward him, and slipped his tongue into her mouth. She felt her gorge coming up, and swallowed it back down.

She said, "I can't really do you properly with this tape on my wrist and ankles, and you like a naughty girl, don't you?"

Randy grinned widely, displaying most of his stained and decaying teeth; Cindy's stomach did a flip. He said to her, "All men like naughty girls, but very few get what they want. So you're telling me, if I take that tape off, this just might be my lucky day?"

She shot him a sly look and said, "I'm a really good naughty girl."

Randy looked uncertain for a moment and said, "If you try anything, I'll call Jeff in here and let him have a go at you. And if you bite me, I'll have a go at you. Do you understand me clearly?"

She said in her husky voice again, "You talk too much, come here, sexy." So, he took the tape off her wrist and ankles. After Cindy had sex with Randy she cuddled up closely to him and whispered, "It can always be like that between the two of us. I've never had a man like you. I want just you. Please don't let your brother wreck it for us. Promise me that I will only be yours."

"Jeff isn't going to like that."

"You can stand up to him, Randy. Make him find another girl. I want to be yours and yours alone."

"I don't know about that, but I can ask him."

"Don't ask him, Randy. You tell him how it is going to be."

"You don't know my big brother very well, nobody tells him anything. He will be the first to tell you, he is the one that does the telling around here."

Cindy ran her hands seductively up and down Randy's arms and said in the same husky voice, "Look at you, Randy, you're so big and strong. No one can tell you to do anything that you don't want to do."

"Jeff has been telling me what to do since I can remember."

"Well, aren't you getting sick and tired of it, Randy?" Cindy wiggled up closer to him and said, "Besides, you have never had a chance at such a prize before have you?"

"The other girls didn't like me like you do." Cindy involuntarily stiffened up and Randy noticed, so he hurriedly added, "I didn't like them either, but I didn't hurt them. Jeff is the one who does that."

Cindy's heart was pounding wildly in her chest and she had a hard time bringing the words to her lips, as she spoke the dreaded question, "What other girls are you talking about, Randy?"

"I didn't kill them, Cindy. I've never killed anyone; I swear to you, I haven't."

Cindy's eyes grew wide in fear and panic, as she started to hyperventilate and to look around the room like a caged animal. She looked at him and was able to focus through her fear that was crushing her as she asked, "Are you talking about all those missing girls over the years?" Randy nodded and reached for her, but she pulled back and said, "Randy, promise me that you will save me? You can do it, Randy. I'll tell you what; I'll distract him and then you can take care of him."

"I love my brother. I can't hurt him."

"But how do you feel about me now, Randy? I bet I'm the only girl who has ever cared about you. Together, we could have the best life, but Jeff doesn't want you to be happy does he, Randy? I bet he killed those other girls because they liked you and not him. He is jealous of you. How can you not see that, Randy? To me, it is as plain as day that all he wants is control over you, just like he does with us girls. He is sick, Randy and, if what you say is true, that you have never killed anyone, then you can get out now, while you still can."

"Well, I don't know, maybe you're right, Cindy."

She snuggled in closer to him and said, "Of course, I'm right. I can be your girl and if you don't want to harm him, then you can just stand up to him, and tell him I'm your girl and that is all there is to it. You can be my great big strong protector," she said, putting her arms around his neck and pulling him into her. She gave him a long lingering kiss. Just then the door flew open, and Jeff came stumbling into the room, waiving the .40 caliber around dangerously in the air.

Jeff's speech was slurred as he said, "We need to get rid of her, Randy."

"Jeff, why do we need to do that? No one is going to find us here."

Jeff leaned drunkenly up against the wall and said, "Like hell they won't find us here. Besides, we're not going to take any chances. No body, no proof that we did a damn thing. Besides, this bitch has the Feds looking for her and, if they find her, they find us. What part of that do you not understand, Randy?"

"I've never killed any of them, Jeff. I'm not going to start now. And anyway, I like this one. She is super-hot, and a lot of fun."

Jeff leered at her, slowly ran his tongue grotesquely over his lips and said, "She sure the hell is hot to trot; I'll give you that, but she's got to go."

"Why can't we just keep her?"

"Where the hell is the fun in keeping them, Randy? Variety is the spice of life. Hell, haven't you learned anything from me, you damn nitwit?"

"I'm not going to kill her."

"Like hell you're not!"

"I said I've never killed any of them."

"That is exactly why you're going to start. You're getting soft on me, Randy. I can't have that."

"Randy, please help me?" Cindy pleaded.

Jeff grinned wickedly at her and mocked her, "Randy, please help me? That is what they all said, because they all thought they could con the nitwit. Cindy, hot-stuff, look at the good it did them. You will never be found, just like the rest of them. Then, to Randy, he said, "You're going to put her in the rowboat, and take her far out on the river, and put a few slugs into her."

Randy stood up, reached down, and grabbed one of Cindy's arms, yanking her to her feet. "Randy, you promised me you would protect me! Why can't you just stand up to him?"

Jeff mumbled, "You just don't get it, sister. Haven't you ever heard of the good cop, and the bad cop scenario? Randy here is the good cop, because all of you think you can con him, and he is the one conning you. He gets the sex the way he likes it. But not me, I'm the bad cop and guess what? I like it rough, really rough, so I get what I like too. With the same girl, two different types of sex; you get the picture? Why on earth would he want to save you? You got suckered, so you see, he isn't as dumb as you thought he was."

Cindy tugged on Randy's arm and pleaded with him, "Please, Randy, please stand up to him before he destroys you." Jeff found this so amusing that he threw back his head and laughed long and hard.

"He is my flesh and blood brother," Randy said, and dragged her out of the cabin, while Jeff stumbled along behind them. The rowboat was resting upon the bank just beyond the edge of the water. The oars rested inside leaning upon the seats. Spider webs crisscrossed all over the boat. It had not been used in a very long time. Once they were all three standing beside the boat, Randy said to her in a very stern voice, "Get in the boat." Cindy looked around with wild frightened eyes. She was looking for any possible escape route. Randy tightened his grip on her arm and pain shot up into her shoulder, and then he shoved her hard toward the rowboat. She stumbled and fell sprawling into the boat.

Jeff chuckled sadistically, and said, "Now, that is a very good girl."

Randy immediately started to shove the boat into the water. Cindy tried to spring up and out of the boat, but Randy grabbed her and hurled her back inside. And then Jeff delivered a blow to her head with the butt of the pistol, and she slumped limply to the bottom of the boat. Jeff sneered and said, "There, now she will be no trouble for a while, little brother. Be sure to wake her up before you shoot her. I want her to feel it. She has brought us a whole lot of trouble with these damn Feds poking around, looking for her. Here, you're going to need this," Jeff said, handing Randy the .40 caliber. Randy took the pistol, climbed into the boat, and used an oar to slide the rowboat farther into the water. An eagle took wing from a nearby tree and made a tight circle in the sky far above them.

Randy braced his legs against the seat in front of him on either side of where Cindy lay upon the bottom of the boat. She was bleeding from a gash upon her forehead where Jeff had struck her with his pistol. Randy felt anger surging up inside him, like heated water surging up from the bottom of a percolator. Anger had been simmering there for years now. He looked at Jeff, who was still standing and watching him from the riverbank, grow smaller and smaller with each pull of the oars. Then, he looked back down at

Cindy, as she lay helpless upon the bottom of the boat. His anger grew, swelling up inside like the festering wound which it was. Jeff wanted to pull Randy all the way to the bottom where Jeff wallowed. Randy had always wanted to be like his big brother, who was so adored by their mother. Randy had taken great pains to win some of her admiration, but what he got instead was left over crumbs. He knew there was no turning back the clock, because this situation was never going to change. Then, along came this girl, who for a fleeting moment in time made him feel like a real man for the first time in his life, because she really was different from the other girls. She seemed to really believe in him, or was she conning him just like Jeff said? Randy's mind was spinning around and around like a broken, out of control Ferris wheel. He put all of his strength into putting as much water between himself and Jeff that he could. But with each dip of the oars into the icy water, his confusion, frustration, and hatred mounted.

Cindy felt dizzy and nauseous and was disoriented when she first opened her eyes. Then, she looked up and saw Randy with an oar in each hand, throwing all his strength into each pull, plowing the rowboat by force through the water. The .40 caliber was tucked into the waistband of his pants. He was staring intently at something, and was not looking at her at that moment. She fixed her eyes on the pistol, and quickly calculated her odds of making a grab for the gun, but the very moment she stirred he looked down at her, fixing his eyes on her, and stared at her coldly. She slowly rose up into a sitting position, and nearly swooned from the movement. She looked around to get her bearings, and she could see Jeff still standing on the riverbank, well behind them now. "Look, Randy, you don't have to do this. We could just keep rowing. My family is very wealthy. They will take care of us. You could turn your bother in, and you will be a local hero for saving me. You didn't commit those other crimes, Jeff did. My grandmother can hire you the best defense attorney that money can buy. She will do that for you, if you save me. I bet there is even a huge amount of reward money offered for my safe return. Randy you could be rich."

"Shut up!"

"But, Randy, don't you see?"

"I said to shut your damned mouth! I have to think."

Cindy reached out and gently touched his leg and he immediately pulled away. When the rowboat was three quarters of the way across the river, Randy set the oars down and said, "This is good." He pulled the .40 caliber from his waistband and said, "Stand up!"

"Randy, I beg of you, please have mercy on me? If you do this there will be no turning back for you. Don't you understand? This is exactly what Jeff wants. He will have even more control over you. Is that what you want? Aren't you already smothering under the weight of his control?"

"Shut the fuck up and stand up!"

Cindy made like she was standing up, but dove into the river in one smooth movement. She sliced through icy river water using her legs to propel her toward the bottom of the river. She heard an explosion of gunfire overhead, and it echoed eerily under the surface, first one shot and then a second shot.

Randy slowly turned his rowboat around, and scanned the surface for any sign of Cindy, and he was satisfied that there was no sign of her anywhere. Muscles all across his back ached with raw tension and his jaw hurt, because he had his teeth clamped down so tightly. He had no idea if he had done the right, or the wrong thing. He hated the uncertainty of not knowing either way. When he finally rowed up to the bank, Jeff stumbled out into the river to help pull in the boat.

Jeff was grinning ear to ear as he said, "Now see, that wasn't so hard, was it little brother?"

Randy glared at him and said, "Just shut the fuck up! I don't want to talk about it."

"I'll tell you, it gets easier and easier with each one."

Randy pointed his gun at Jeff and said, "You say another word about it, and I'll blow your damn head right off your shoulders! Do you understand me?"

Jeff held his hands up defensively and said, "Hey, take it easy, little brother, I meant no harm." He took the bottle of rum out from the waistband of his pants and extended it to Randy.

Randy turned the bottle up and chugged down the remaining rum, and then slung the empty bottle into the river. Jeff grinned and said, "In the river with the rest of the trash." Randy glared at Jeff again, and said nothing as he turned and walked back up toward their cabin.

When Jeff stumbled into the cabin, Randy grabbed Jeff by his throat and pinned him up against the wall with one hand. In his other hand Randy held an envelope stuffed full of one hundred dollar bills in Jeff's face. "When the fuck were you going to tell me about this, huh, big brother? You're doing shit behind my back. You're getting me involved, and then you're trying to double cross me? When were you going to tell me, huh?" Spittle flew into Jeff's face, as Randy screeched at him.

"Honestly, I was going to tell you all about that money!"

"Like hell you were!"

"I was, I swear, I was going to tell you."

"Well, now that you have my attention, I suggest you start talking. I'm all ears," Randy said, grinning wickedly, as he tightened his hold on Jeff's throat.

Jeff choked, and whispered in a raspy voice, "I can't, I can't breathe."

Randy grinned again wickedly, and squeezed his hand around Jeff's throat tighter, until he saw Jeff's eyes widen in terror. A wide smile of sadistic satisfaction spread across Randy's face as he ever so slightly loosened his grip. "I said, I'm all ears, are you fucking deaf?"

"It is payment for a job."

"What kind of job, Jeff? What the fuck did you get us into this time? What kind of job do we have to do to make this kind of money?"

"You just did the job, Randy?"

Randy dug the nose of the .40 into Jeff's left temple, "What the fuck are you talking about?"

"That girl, she was what the money was for."

"You fucking set me up for a hit that I didn't know anything about? You cocksucker! I should just blow your brains out all over this wall!"

"Randy, no don't do it, please? When Ma is gone, we will only have each other."

"Right now, I'm thinking Cindy was right all along. I would be better off without you dragging me down into hell with you!"

"Randy, look, I'll give you all the money. It is yours, every bit of it."

"Who paid you, Jeff? Who else knows about this?"

Chapter 8

Chad pulled out of Miss Newton's driveway and headed back to Weaverville. Once he was back in town, he pulled up in front of the sheriff's office. Chad walked into the building and found Sheriff Marker sitting behind his desk. The sheriff rose up from his chair and extended his hand out to Chad and said, "It is good to see you again, Agent Turner. "What can I do for you?"

Chad shook Sheriff Marker's hand, and the sheriff motioned to a chair across from his desk and said, "Please have a seat."

Chad sat down and said, "Sheriff, I understand that you and your deputies do regular patrols of Mrs. Porter's businesses?"

"Yes we do, as with all businesses here in town."

"May I get a copy of your regular patrol log and a copy of all reports from the night Cindy Porter was abducted?"

Sheriff Marker said hesitantly, "Sure, I can make that happen. May I ask why you're interested in the information?"

Chad shrugged casually and replied, "It is just so I can get a feel for the day to day business routine here in Weaverville."

"Hey, we tracked down Tim Walker for you."

"Yeah, what did you find out?"

"He fell off the wagon. He had been sober for years. He left town and had a real party. It appears he didn't want his shack-up job to know."

Chad smiled and said, "People never cease to amaze me."

"How is that?"

"Here she is an obvious drug user, and he doesn't want her to know he drinks?"

Sheriff Marker smiled and said, "If this world made any sense, no one would need us, Agent Turner."

Chad said casually, "Oh, by the way, we're putting out an APB on two young gentlemen, which we want to bring in for questioning in Cindy Porter's abduction."

Sheriff Marker's lips turned up at the corners into a predatory smile, and he leaned closer into his desk, "Saving the best for last? What the hell have you come up with?"

"Not enough yet, Sheriff, we're just trying to rule folks in or out as we find them."

"I'm too damn old for you to try to play coy with me, Agent Turner."

Chad pushed back his chair and stood up. "Your office will be receiving the information very shortly. About those logs, how soon can I expect to have them?"

"I'll have my dispatcher pull it up and send you the file tonight. Is that soon enough to suit you?" The change in Sheriff Marker's demeanor and tone was not lost on Chad. Chad thought this man and Cindy's mother had much in common. "You know, Mrs. Porter Sr. is calling me daily, demanding to know what progress we're making! You're not being helpful!"

"My job here is to bring this girl home. How much more helpful can that be Sheriff? Now, if you will excuse me?"

"Look, I'm sorry; I'm just under a lot of pressure here."

"I can only imagine," Chad said, and left the office. Sheriff Marker was nothing more than Mrs. Porter Sr.'s puppet, just as Karen had said, and that was clear.

Later in the evening, just as Sheriff Marker had promised, Chad received the log of the weekly patrols. Chad sat down and got busy mapping out the Porter businesses in town. Sure enough, just as Karen had pointed out, a hugely disproportionate percentage of all patrols went to Porter businesses. On the evening of Cindy Porter's abduction, a patrol car was scheduled to pass Porter's Stop and Go at the exact time of her abduction, just as Chad expected. From a law enforcements perspective, it made good sense to be patrolling an area, just as a business was scheduled to close. This is why he also requested the call logs from Sheriff Marker.

Chad saw that, on the evening of Cindy Porter's abduction, an interesting deviation to an otherwise routine schedule occurred. What was even more interesting was, it occurred just slightly before the abduction happened. The patrol which was usually in the close vicinity of Porter's Stop and Go was diverted to another call of a possible prowler at none other than Mrs. Porter Sr.'s residence. If Chad had not asked to see the patrol logs for that evening of the abduction, he would not have known this diversion had occurred.

Since there were two abductors on the video and one prowler at the residence, this was what appeared to Chad to be a very well-planned and coordinated effort, with not two but three suspects. Chad was starting to feel less confident about these two brothers as likely suspects, unless they had a third partner. The prowler, Chad was sure, was no coincidence. This seemed to be totally lost on Sheriff Marker who, by all accounts, was a well-seasoned officer.

Chad's cell rang, "Turner here."

"Chad, this is Bruce Whipply. The guys who put a tap on Miss Newton's phone for you haven't picked up any activity yet, but they did run a check on the last activity for a cell phone which belongs to Jeff Newton. The last ping that has been picked up from his cell phone was from a cell tower near Badger River Wilderness Preserve. The first ping was at 2:18 pm and it pinged at regular intervals from the same tower, until just up to a half hour ago."

"Bruce, 2:18 was just about the time I left Miss Newton's yard. It seems momma bear got a hold of her cubs before we could get our tap into place. Can you get me the exact coordinates of the cell tower?"

"I will email it to you right now. My guess is that phone was ditched."

Chad leaned back in his chair and said, "I'm guessing you're right, but that, in and of itself, makes me happy. I'm going to have to put a call in for those phone records. I want to know whom else those punks have been talking to." Chad was hoping the records could possibly lead to the third suspect, the prowler.

"You may not be so happy when you try to find them out there in backwoods country, without a cell phone to track their whereabouts."

Chad smiled and said, "Now Whipply, just how many cell towers do you think could possibly be out in a wilderness preserve?"

"It's not the wilderness preserve I'm talking about. They have to come out sometime, and when they do, it sure would be nice to know it, don't you agree? So why are you happy they threw the phone away?"

"Because, Whipply, in my mind, it moves them up higher on my list of possible suspects. How far is this wilderness preserve from Elk?"

"It is just outside of Elk. Hell that town of Elk, if you can call it a town, looked pretty much like a wilderness area to me."

"That is perfect!"

"OK, now you've got me again, why is it perfect?"

"It is perfect; because Miss Newton told me her sons have a fort of some type in those woods. My guess is, if we can find their fort, we can find them."

"Did she give you any idea where it is?"

"No, because, I don't think she knows where it is. But, I don't think she would tell me, even if she did know. I will take a drive out that way tomorrow."

The very next morning, Chad drove out to Badger River Wilderness Preserve, using the coordinates which Bruce Whipply had given him. Chad backed his car up off the roadway, where it was mostly hidden from view. Chad sat there for a bit and looked around in complete silence. It was not long before a deer ambled out of the trees and calmly sauntered across the rural roadway. A scrub jay enthusiastically announced the deer's presence. Chad was just about to turn on his engine and drive deeper into the wilderness preserve, when a white Honda sped around a turn. Curious, Chad followed the car, but he hung back out of their sight. Once they got onto a more populated section of the highway, Chad picked up his speed and gained on them, but he still hung back, but now he could keep them in sight without alerting them. He had no idea who was in the car, and he was hoping to get close enough to run its plates. He waited until they reached the little town of Elk, before he tried to close in on them. Incredulously, the driver of the white Honda made an evasive maneuver with his car, which sent another car head-on into Chad's vehicle. As Chad watched helplessly, the white Honda raced away from the crash site. "Son of a bitch," Chad said, as he reached for his cell phone and called Sheriff Marker.

People from the other car approached Chad's window and were banging on it. Chad flashed his badge at them and then ignored them, while he waited for Sheriff Marker to answer.

Finally, Sheriff Marker picked up the call. "This is, Sheriff Marker, speaking."

"Sheriff, this is Chad Turner. Could you ask the highway patrol here around Elk to put up roadblocks within a fifty mile radius of Elk, and issue an APB on an older white Honda Accord; the year of the vehicle is 2001 to possibly 2003? Its license plate number is currently unknown. It has two Caucasian male suspects in the vehicle, who are possibly Jeff and Randy Newton, and they are considered armed and dangerous.

Could you also coordinate with the surrounding counties law enforcement agencies, within a one hundred mile radius, and ask for all available officers for a manhunt? I will confirm with Elk PD, that our command center will be police headquarters in Elk. I see no problem with getting it approved by them; after all, they have a dog in this fight."

"This is an exciting development, Agent Turner. I will let Mrs. Porter Sr. know."

"The roadblocks are urgent, Sheriff Marker."

Sheriff Marker was taken aback by Chad's comment, but he simply replied, "I understand. I will get right on it."

"Thank you. I'm putting in a call right now to secure additional resources from my people. Let everyone know to be at Elk Police Station at 7:00 a.m. sharp," Chad said.

"I will do that."

"Thank you, Sheriff, I will be in touch." Next, Chad called Dan Anderson's number.

Dan picked up the call, "Anderson, here."

"Dan, our suspects have been located. I need all hands on board."

"What the hell does that mean, Turner?"

"Everything you can send my way, ASAP. And a bird would be a nice plus."

"I don't have a helicopter available right this second. How about a drone, will that do?"

"I'll take it, along with every sharpshooter that you can get your hands on. Also I want a tracker."

"You've already got access to dog teams."

"I also want a tracker, and the best one you have, with no exceptions. If the tracker is on another case, pull them off of it. I'm not going to lose these suspects, if they manage to get back into the wilderness preserve, which was their boyhood retreat. The odds are in their favor and I want to put a tight squeeze on those two.

"Do you know what an operation like this is going to cost?"

"Dan, those are two monsters running lose in these woods, and young women are dying and have been for years. They're not going to stop, until we stop them. And quite frankly, Dan, I don't give a shit about your budget."

"It is always a pleasure working with you, Chad, because you're always so charming. Your teams will be deployed as soon as we hang up but, because of the logistics of having equipment airlifted to you, engage as much surrounding law enforcement that you can muster up in the meantime. Let them burn some of their resources on this."

"That was my first phone call, Dan, but it is my resources that are going to find this girl. Also, Dan, add another unmarked car to my order, because mine is going to be out of commission for a spell."

Dan said, "Oh, why the hell not!"

"Thank you, Dan. I will be in touch," Chad said and ended the call. By that time, a police car was on the scene of the accident. Chad asked the officer to have his station issue Chad another unmarked car, until his new one arrived with the other provisions for the manhunt. Finally, Chad exchanged required information with the other motorist who was a bit more than pissed off. Next, Chad placed a call to the Elk Chief of Police and told him that he needed a war-room set up at the Elk station by 7:00 a.m. the following morning. Chad also requested any manpower the chief could spare. Chad told him that Sheriff Marker would also be calling him about the same request. Chad was told they had a large conference room, and its schedule would be wiped clean for as long as necessary.

Right after Sheriff Marker got off his call with the Highway Patrol, concerning roadblocks and asking for any resources they could provide to be at Elk Police Station at 7:00 am, he called Mrs. Porter Sr.

The phone rang several times, before a raspy voice answered. Someone who was not familiar with Mrs. Porter Sr.'s voice could have easily mistaken it for a man's voice. "Hello?"

"Mrs. Porter, this is Sheriff Marker."

"I know it is you. I hope you have something worthwhile to say about this investigation, Sheriff. After all, it is high time that we have some results. That is my Granddaughter out there somewhere, you know?"

"Mrs. Porter, you know we have had people working on this almost around the clock."

"Almost isn't good enough, Sheriff. You and I both know the first few hours are crucial and this has dragged into days. If anything happens to my granddaughter, heads are going to roll, and trust me when I say; I will start at the very top."

"We have a lead on a few possible suspects."

"Well, why the hell didn't you spit it out?"

"I've been trying."

"Well, who the hell are they, and when are you going to drag their asses in for questioning?"

"We have to find them first."

"What the hell do you mean that you have to find them first? Why, in God's name, are you wasting your time talking on this phone to me? You need to get your ass out there and find them!"

"You asked me to keep you apprised of everything that is going on." Mrs. Porter slammed the handset down upon the receiver before he could finish. He sighed; he thought the old bitch would be happy they were finally making some kind of progress in this case. He looked up from his desk, and saw the dispatcher was grinning at him. "What the hell are you smiling about?"

"Nothing Sheriff, I was just taking a bit of a break."

"Well, get your ass back to work. I want you to find out exactly where the CHP is setting up those roadblocks. You take too many breaks, as far as I'm concerned," Sheriff Marker said, as he walked out of the office and slammed the door behind him."

Chapter 9

It was well past midnight and Miss Newton was sound asleep, when a hand reached out of the darkness, touching her shoulder. Her eyes flew open in panic, and her heart went into a blood pumping frenzy. She instinctively reached for a butcher knife she kept under her other pillow. A voice came out of the darkness in a whisper, "Ma, Ma, it is me, Jeff."

Miss Newton sat up in her bed and reached for a lamp on her nightstand. The same hand that had touched her shoulder clamped down upon her wrist. Jeff whispered again, "We can't turn on lights, because I'm sure they're watching our house."

Miss Newton hissed, "Then what the hell are you doing here? You're trying to drag my ass into whatever the hell it is that you and your dimwit brother have gotten into."

"Ma, I came to get some more canned food. We can't keep coming here, because it is too risky. We need you to go grocery shopping, and stash food every week out in the bushes behind the sign for Badger River Wildness Preserve."

"Like hell I'm going to do that! I thought your brother was the only dimwit that I gave birth to. Don't you think they're going to put a tail on me? They're going to be expecting me to help you, if they think you're still in this area."

"You've got to help us, Ma!"

"I don't have to do any damn such thing! You two have gotten yourselves into this. You're just going to have to figure out another way to get food. You can come here for it, but if you get caught, I'll claim you were here robbing me. I'm not spending the rest of my life in a cell for the likes of you two. I've already given up the best years of my life for you two and that no count who fathered you both.

Does this have anything to do with that missing girl who has been plastered all over the news? If you have her, you sure as hell better let her go, you dumbass."

"I don't know what this has to do with, Ma. I swear I don't know why the FBI or anyone else would be looking for us. We're hiding because we're scared that we could be framed for something we did not do."

His mother stared at him incredulously in the dark room and said, "You really think I'm stupid, don't you?"

"No, Ma, of course, I don't think you're stupid."

"Get your damned food, and get the hell out of here. Where is your brother? Watching that damned girl, I'll bet!"

"No, Ma. I told you we don't have a girl. He is waiting for me at the car."

"Well now, get your food and go on and get. You make me nervous just being here."

Jeff rummaged around in his mother's pantry, filling up a box with random cans of food in the dark. He had no idea what he was putting into the box, because he didn't dare turn on lights, because he knew their house was being watched. When he finished filling the box, he climbed out the open window in which he had entered. Dark clouds covered the moon as he silently slipped back into the surrounding woods, with all the stealth of a panther stalking prey.

When Jeff returned to the car, he found Randy pacing back and forth. "What in the hell took you so damn long? I was just about ready to take off without you."

"Well, you had better be happy you didn't, because, if you ever do that to me, I will kill you, when I catch up to you."

"Let's get the hell out of here," Randy said, jumping behind the wheel.

Jeff put the groceries on the backseat of the car, and got in. Randy left the headlights off, until they were well away from the area where their mother lived, even though they had come in on an old logging road, which was well out of sight from her house. They could not afford to take any chances. They rode in silence for a while, and then Jeff said, "Ma said she is not going to get groceries for us. She said we're on our own."

"Why is she being such a bitch?"

"She is worried they will place a tail on her, and she doesn't want to go down with us if we get caught."

Randy glanced over at his older brother and said, "What the hell are we going to do now?"

"We will just have to break into homes and steal grub when we need to. That will be pretty easy; it just involves more effort on our part. Also, we need to get another ride as soon as some of this heat dies down.

As they approached Badger River Wilderness Preserve, Randy saw a roadblock up ahead, "What the fuck is this?"

"Turn around and gun it! Hurry up, damn it!" Jeff said.

Randy slammed their car into reverse, and they made a run for it, but cop cars seemed to just appear out of the darkness. Randy was swerving, trying to get around them, and then his car hit a tire spike, which had been laid down on the roadway. Randy barely had time to comprehend everything that was happening, because it was all coming so fast at him. Then, bullets started flying; he couldn't believe that Jeff was shooting at the cops, until he saw a cop car swerve and go off the road, plowing through some undergrowth beside the road. To Randy, everything seemed to be surreal and happening in slow motion as he saw Jeff, with his gun blazing, throw open the passenger door and leap from it, tumbling over the embankment toward Badger River. Randy was lost emotionally, and he didn't know what else to do, so he simply stopped the car and put his hands in the air.

Randy heard a command come over a loud speaker from one of the squad cars; "Step away from your vehicle, with your hands in the air." Randy opened his door and stepped out, with his hands held high over his head. The next thing he knew, he was knocked to the ground, with such force that air was knocked from his lungs and he struggled to catch his breath, but couldn't because he had a mound of police officers on top of him compressing his lungs. Out of self-preservation, he struggled to get free, not because he was resisting arrest, but, because he simply could not breathe. He was beaten with billy clubs until he lost conscious.

When Sheriff Marker got word they had a suspect in custody, he eagerly called Mrs. Porter Sr.

She answered on the first ring, "Hello?"

"Mrs. Porter, it is me, Sheriff Marker. I have some great news for you."

"You have found Cindy?"

"No, I'm sorry to say, we haven't found her quite yet, but we have a suspect in custody."

"What did he say?"

"I don't know what he has said yet. They just brought him into the Elk Police Station."

"Well then, you had better get your ass over there! I want a firsthand account. I want to know everything he says, and I want nothing left out. Take notes, if you need to."

"Mrs. Porter, it is out of my jurisdiction."

"I don't give a rat's ass, if it is out of your jurisdiction or not, you figure out a way to get into that room. I want to hear every detail. Do I make myself clearly understood?"

"Yes, ma'am, I will figure something out, I'm on my way."

"Good, I want to hear the moment that you hear anything significant."

"Yes, Mrs. Porter, I understand. I will be in touch with you very soon, goodbye." She hung up, without responding.

When Randy regained consciousness, he was handcuffed, with his hands behind his back, and he was laying on the backseat of a squad car. Red lights streaked through the night air in front of him and behind him. He sat up and could see other police cars racing past them, with their lights flashing and sirens piercing the night sky. Other squad cars were rushing toward Badger River Wilderness Preserve. The squad car that he was riding in was heading back toward town. His head pounded, and his left eye burned like hell and was leaking tears down that side of his face. He tried to keep his eye closed, because it hurt so much worse open. There were two boys in blue in the front seats. The cop which was driving glanced in his review mirror and said, "Look who is awake."

The other cop turned around and asked Randy, "Did you have a nice little nap?" Both cops chuckled, and the one in the passenger seat said, "Oh, what happened to your eye?" Then there was another round of laughter from the cops. When they arrived at Elk Police Station, the same two police officers read Randy his rights, flanked him on either side, and escorted him into an interrogation room. There was already another man in a dark blue suit, with eyes almost the exact color as the suit, standing in the room at one end of a long table. Randy suspected right away this guy must be a federal agent, because he simply didn't look like he fit in this locale. His suit was finely tailored, his grooming was impeccable, and just everything about him screamed big city.

The man nodded at the two police officers, who had escorted Randy into the room, "Thank you, gentlemen, I will take it from here." The man waited until the two police officers had cleared the room before he spoke to Randy. "I'm Special Agent Chad Turner, with the Federal Bureau of Investigation, and I would like to ask you a few questions regarding the disappearance of Cindy Porter."

"I don't know any Cindy Porter, and I don't have a clue why your baboons jumped me."

"Can you tell me then, Mr. Newton, why the gentleman in the car you were driving was firing a weapon at law enforcement, and why you were trying to avoid a roadblock?"

"Jeff told me to back up, turn around, and punch it."

"That would be Jeff Newton your bother, I take it?"

"Look, you can take it and shove it up your ass! I don't know anything, and you can't make me talk about something I don't know about!"

"If Cindy Porter is still alive, and we find her in time, you just might be able to avoid the death penalty. Especially, if you turn state's witness, and tell us what really happened to her and the other missing girls?"

"I told you, that I don't know anything about any missing girls. You're not going to frame me for anything."

"When you tried to avoid our roadblock tonight, where were you going, Randy?"

"We were just driving around, looking for something to do. There isn't any law against that is there?"

"You were just driving around out in Badger River Wilderness Preserve at night? There is not much to do this time of night out there, is there, Randy? Or maybe, Randy, just maybe, you two have something of interest tucked away out there?"

"We were just driving, I told you."

"Your mother told me that you and your brother have a fort in the woods there."

"Ma told you that?"

"Yes she did, Randy. Apparently, you two have had a fort there for a few years now."

"Ma doesn't know shit! We never tell her the truth about anything."

"Your mother knows more than you think she does. According to her, both of you started spending more and more time at your fort and cutting school right about the time the first girl went missing right here in Elk."

"Why the hell would she tell you something stupid like that?"

Chad shrugged nonchalantly, "I don't know, Randy. Why would she say something like that?"

"She's an old bitch. She gets mixed up and all turned around."

"Well that could be, Randy, but it is easy enough to confirm whether she is correct or not, with school records for both you and your brother."

"We cut school all the time, so records don't mean a damn thing."

"If your delinquency dramatically increased with the disappearance of the first girl, your school records will speak volumes. That is the kind of stuff prosecutors love to feed to a jury. Have you ever been in prison before, Randy?"

"Of course I haven't, because I haven't ever done anything wrong."

Chad pulled out a chair from the table and sat down across from Randy. Narrowing his eyes, Chad leaned toward Randy and gave Randy a hard stare.

"What the fuck are you looking at, you freak?" Randy said, squirming in his seat.

"Randy, wouldn't it be more appropriate to say you haven't been to prison yet, because you and Jeff haven't been caught before now?"

"I tried to avoid a roadblock. You don't have anything else on me. You can't send me to prison for that. You're just trying to scare me! I'll tell you something, Mr. hot shit FBI Man, it isn't working. Oh wait, I was driving a stolen car, big whoopee doo!"

"Randy, let me ask you this. Where were you on September sixth, at 11:30 pm?"

"I was with my brother, probably. How the hell should I know where I was then?"

"Randy, it was only this last week? Are you telling me that you can't remember? Let me be clearer. It was this last Friday night."

"So, what about it, why do you want to know?"

"It was the night Porter's Stop and Go was robbed, and Miss Cindy Porter was abducted."

"Like I told you, I was with my brother. We always hang out together."

"Where were you hanging out? Can anyone besides your brother verify you two were not at Porter's Stop and Go at that time?"

"Sure, Ma, can verify it for us, because we were just hanging out at home Friday night. Now I remember! We were at home, because we didn't have anything to do."

"Randy, your mother told me the last time she saw either one of you was approximately noon on September sixth, so I don't think that alibi is going to fly."

"You're lying to me! You're just trying to trick me into saying something that will incriminate me. I want to see a lawyer!"

Just then, there was a rap on the door. Politely, Chad said, "Please excuse me for a moment." Chad could see through a small window in the door that Sheriff Marker was standing on the other side. Sheriff Marker's timing couldn't have been more perfect as far as Chad was concerned. Chad stepped out into the hallway and motioned for the officer, who was waiting right outside of the door, to step into the room to guard Randy Newton in Chad's absence. "Hello, Sheriff, what brings you all the way over here at this late hour of night?"

Sheriff Marker lied to Chad, "I just caught wind that you guys have already apprehended one of the suspects. And since Cindy's abduction occurred in my jurisdiction, I thought maybe you wouldn't mind if I sit in on a bit of the interrogation? I promise I will not get in your way. I just think people in my community would be happy to feel that I'm on top of things."

Chad could totally see right through Sheriff Marker's comment, but Chad let it slide. Chad filled Sheriff Marker in on what Chad's next tactic was going to be, because Chad needed Sheriff Marker to play a role in it. The sheriff was very excited that he got to play an active role, because this was going to please Mrs. Porter Sr. immensely, if their ploy worked. Together, the two men entered the room and relieved the guard of his post for the time being. Chad smiled and said, "Randy, I'm sure you have been very worried about your big brother, seeing how he was shooting at local law enforcement. Hell, you must have been worried he was trying suicide by cop, or something stupid like that?"

Randy's brows furrowed and he said, "What the hell are you trying to say? Don't play with me, you bastard!"

"Oh, I wouldn't dream of playing with you, Randy. I'll let you hear it from Sheriff Marker for yourself. Go ahead and fill him in Sheriff."

"We just captured Jeff a little while ago. I'm happy to say he wants to turn state's witness for a plea deal. He is already singing like a canary."

"You're lying! Jeff would never do that! We have a deal. My brother would never double-cross me."

Sheriff Marker grinned broadly and rocked back on the heels of his cowboy boots and said, "He has already ratted you out. He said you're the one who took Cindy. Hell, he said you took all those girls. He said he kept begging you to let them go."

"That is a blatant lie! Let me see him, because I don't even believe you have him."

Chad said, "Now, Randy, it doesn't really matter to us what you believe. What does matter is we keep Jeff talking to us, since you have not been cooperative at all. You seem to have this brotherly love thing going on, and Jeff is clearly uninhibited by that."

Sheriff Marker spoke up and added, "You see, Randy, at this point in time, we don't really need you at all. We're just trying to give you an opportunity to set the record straight, to defend yourself, because Jeff is trying to bury you. Trust me, when I say, if I was in your shoes and didn't do these heinous things, which Jeff is saying you did, I would want everyone to know it."

Beads of sweat began to seep out the pores upon Randy's brow, and his whole body tensed up as he nervously squirmed in his chair. He hated to have to make decisions. He felt these guys were lying; after all, they were cops, and therefore could never be trusted under any circumstances as far as he was concerned. Hell, even his mother had drilled that into him. And Jeff had spent years reinforcing what Randy's mother had taught them. But there was this nagging feeling surging up in his gut that they may really have Jeff, and they seemed to know too damn much. How could they possibly know about the girls? He knew Jeff wanted him to kill Cindy, so Jeff could have something to hang over Randy's head for more control over him, just like Cindy had said. So here it was; this was Jeff's way out, while laying all the blame at Randy's feet. "I did not kill any of those girls."

Chad felt that this was the sweet spot. The place in a moment in time which made him love the shit out of this job. Chad sat down on a chair again across from Randy and leaned in trying his damnedest to not look excited. Chad coolly asked, "Randy, why do you think we would be willing to take your word over Jeff's? You have not been cooperative with us at all, until we backed you into the proverbial corner."

"It is the truth; I'm telling you. Jeff wanted me to kill Cindy, but I didn't."

Sheriff Marker blurted out, "Where is she, Randy?"

Randy looked up at Sheriff Marker and said, "She was in the river the last time I saw her."

Chad asked Randy, "Is she alive?"

Tears welled up in Randy's eyes and he answered, "I don't know."

Chad said, "Randy, why was she in the river?"

"She was in the river because Jeff told me to take her way out there in our rowboat and shoot her."

Chad asked, "But you didn't shoot her?"

"No, I don't think so. I took out my gun, and she dove into the water. I had to make it look good, because Jeff was watching from the shore. I fired into the water in the direction she dove in and I was trying to miss her, but I couldn't see where she was for certain." Tears began to leak from his eyes and made little rivulets as they coursed their way through stubble on his unshaved face.

"That is a pretty wide river, Randy. She could have drowned, even if she had not been shot," Chad said.

"I rowed out as close to the other shore as I could, without making Jeff suspicious of what I was really doing. I wanted to get her close enough so she did have a chance. I knew Jeff would kill me, if he knew I let her go."

"But, you don't know that you did let her go, even if that was your intent. If she was shot or drowned, Randy, I'm afraid the outcome is going to be the same for you and your brother," Sheriff Marker said.

Randy looked up at the sheriff, and said, with a quivering chin, "I liked her, Sheriff. I just have a gut feeling she is out there somewhere. I didn't hurt her. I swear I didn't hurt her."

Chad had no idea if Randy was telling the truth or not. Sure, the raw emotions were there, but Chad's experience had taught him well. Usually, these suspects were crying because they got caught. They were almost always too narcissistic to even relate to their victims as fellow human beings. To a narcissistic killer, their victims were just viewed as objects to release whatever pent up emotional need a perpetrator had at the time. Too often, over the course of his years in this field of work, Chad had seen these vile individuals casually shrug, and say their victims were simply in the wrong place at the wrong time. It was usually a totally random process for a perpetrator. Chad said, "Randy, can you show us where this fort of yours is in the woods? That is where you had Cindy, is it not?"

"You're going to let me be the state's witness, if I show you?"

There it was, Chad thought. It was not out of concern for Cindy that Randy may be willing to show them where the location was. It was for what deal Randy could get cut to save his own ass. "I will see what I can do for you, Randy, if you're telling the truth." Chad could not believe his eyes when he saw Randy smile. That smile made Chad's skin crawl. Chad said, "Can you take us out there right now?"

"Hell yes, I can. I know those woods like the back of my hand."

That was exactly what Chad was afraid of. Looking for Jeff in those woods would be like looking for the proverbial needle in a haystack without the high tech equipment and the tracker Dan was sending the next day. Chad knew that all the manpower they had looking for Jeff tonight was just spinning wheels. The only thing that could possibly be gained by the hunt going on right at that moment was the possibility of keeping Jeff on the move and wearing him down.

Chad looked at Sheriff Marker and asked, "Do you want to accompany us out to Badger Wilderness Preserve tonight?"

Sheriff Marker grinned and said, "Hell yes, I do."

Chapter 10

Chad got up from his chair, "Let me see how many officers I can get from here to accompany us. They're pretty busy tonight chasing after Jeff." Chad stepped out into the hallway and asked the guard at the door to summon his shift commander. Chad reentered the room and stood staring hard at Randy.

Randy squirmed again on his chair under Chad's harsh gaze. "I didn't kill any of those girls. I swear I didn't!"

Sheriff Marker said gloating, "We're going to find out if you killed any of those girls or not. We never take a scumbag's word for anything. Hell, you can't even tell us if Cindy is alive, or not."

Soon there was a rap on the door and then it swung open. The shift commander stepped into the room, closing the door behind him. "Look, my resources are stretched pretty thin tonight. The most I can give you is two guys right now. I can't pull any off our search for the other Newton. He fired on my officers. I hope you understand."

"I understand completely. I'll take them, and I'm grateful to have them," Chad said. "We would like to head out immediately, if possible?"

"I will send them in here for you right away."

"That will be excellent. Thank you, sir," Chad said. The commander simply nodded and left the room.

"You bastards just fucking lied to me! You don't have Jeff at all. I'm not taking you anywhere!"

Sheriff Marker smiled like a Cheshire cat and said, "Oh, you're going to take us out there tonight, Randy. After the confession you just gave us, I would think that you would be damn happy to take us out there, and you had better start praying to God that Cindy is still alive, because she may be the only hope in hell you have to prove what you're saying may be true."

"What about my plea deal?" Randy demanded.

Chad looked at Randy and realized he wasn't as dumb as Chad thought. Chad had to come up with something quickly. "I will put it into my report that you're working cooperatively with law enforcement in this urgent matter, as part of an impending plea deal."

"Don't give me any of this impending shit. We either have a plea deal, or we don't!"

"We don't have time for attorneys right now, Einstein!" Sheriff Marker said, stepping toward Randy aggressively.

Chad held up a hand toward Sheriff Marker, "Randy has a right to ask for reassurance. Randy, I will write out a note and sign it for you. It will state, because of your complete cooperation, a plea deal is highly recommended for you. It will be formalized tomorrow when you turn state's witness. Under the circumstance, that is the best I can do for you tonight. Is that fair enough?" Randy thought about this for a long moment and finally shook his head in agreement. Chad stepped from the room and wrote the note. He then asked a clerk to type it up for him. When he took it back to the room, two officers were already there waiting for him. He signed the note and slid it across the table for Randy to sign. Randy took a long while to read the note, and then he reread it before signing it.

"I want my own copy of this."

Rolling his eyes, Sheriff Marker picked up the note and handed it to one of the officers and said, "Would you please carry out our prisoner's request?"

"Yes, sir," the officer said.

As soon as the officer came back with two copies, Chad said, "Let's do this." Sheriff Marker drove his cruiser, with Chad riding along with him. They had Randy on the backseat, with his hands securely cuffed behind his back. Lights of the tiny town slipped away behind them, as their headlights sliced through darkness. Moonlight waxed now and again only to wane back behind dark clouds overhead. The only comfort came from headlights of the other cruiser slightly behind them. Tall dark trees of the forest did little to comfort the three individuals riding in the car. As their headlights swept over the road sign for Badger Creek Wilderness Preserve, a huge owl, which had been perched on the sign, took wing. Its enormous wingspan did nothing to lighten their mood inside the cruiser. Soon, they passed a string of police vehicles parked alongside the road. The search for Jeff was still in full swing.

Chad turned in his seat and said, "Randy, can you tell us what happened the night Cindy was abducted?"

Randy recounted in detail to Chad and Sheriff Marker what really transpired on that dark Friday night.

Randy stood outside the convenience store's rear door. His palms were damp with perspiration, in spite of frigid temperatures of that dark autumn night. He looked up at his brother Jeff. Jeff's face was mostly hidden by a black ski mask pulled down over his head. Jeff's warm breath billowed out of his nostrils like steam on a steam engine, coming in rapid giant puffs. Jeff gripped the handle of his .40 caliber tighter when Randy nodded at him. They both saw the doorknob start to rotate. Cindy, the store clerk, stepped out into the dark night and was immediately knocked to the ground. She was trying franticly to grasp what was happening, when she felt the cold hard steal of a gun barrel press hard against her temple. Jeff stood straddled over the top of her, "Where the hell is it?" he demanded, pressing his gun barrel even harder into her temple.

With her voice trembling in fear, Cindy said, "It's stuffed into the back of my jeans." Jeff nodded to Randy. On cue, Randy reached down and pulled up her jacket and snatched a black money bag from her jeans.

"Where are your car keys?" Jeff demanded. Cindy opened her still clinched hand and held the car keys out to him.

"What the hell do we need with her car keys?" Randy asked in a panicked voice.

Jeff pulled a roll of duct tape out of his jacket, handed it to Randy, and said, "Duct tape her."

"Let's just get the hell out of here, before someone comes, Jeff."

"I said duct tape her, you damn moron. She looks like a fun play toy to me."

"Please, just let me go? I didn't see anything. Please, just take the money and my car?"

"Duct tape her mouth," Jeff told Randy. When Randy was finished with the duct tape, they carried Cindy to her car, tossed her in the trunk, and slammed down the lid. Jeff smiled at Randy and said, "You take our truck, and I'll drive this." Randy ran to their truck and pulled out of the parking lot, while he nervously glanced up and down the street. He had to resist an urge to put the gas pedal to the floor. He saw Jeff pull out of the parking lot in the clerks blue Ford and fall in behind his truck. Randy let out a sigh of relief, when they finally reached an exit to the highway.

Cindy struggled to be free from the duct tape which held her wrists and ankles bound. She was breathing so fast that she was hyperventilating, and she felt dizzy. She had to try to calm down, so she could think. She could hear other cars passing by them on the road. She looked around inside her dark trunk. She still had her cell phone in her back pocket of her jeans. She rolled over onto her side and tried to wiggle it out of her pocket. Her hands were bound back to back, so it was difficult for her to maneuver them the way she needed to. After a long while, she was able to pull the phone from her pocket and slide it open. She tried to guess where the numbers for 911 were, and then she dropped it. She looked around in a panic and could faintly make out through the taillights of her car other headlights coming up behind them on the highway. She frantically scooted toward the rear of the trunk and managed to kick out one of the taillights. A highway patrol car quickly gained on the blue Ford and put on its lights to pull it over. Jeff gripped the steering wheel, until his knuckles turned white, as he quickly calculated what his options were. He pulled over onto the roadside.

Randy saw lights from a highway patrol car and saw Jeff pull off to the shoulder of the road from his rearview mirror. Randy slowed his truck and did a wide U-turn on the highway and doubled back. The officer was just approaching the car, when Randy slowed his truck and said, "What seems to be the problem, officer?" The officer heard Cindy kicking in the trunk just then, and reached for his service weapon, but it was too late for him. Randy offered just enough distraction to allow Jeff to plant a .40 caliber slug into the officer's brain, blowing off the back of his head. Jeff pulled back out onto the highway and Randy followed. Because of Jeff, they now had a dead cop, and a kidnapped store clerk; it was just supposed to be a simple robbery. Randy shook his head in disgust. Jeff had a way of just sucking Randy further and further in. It had always been that way the whole while they were growing up. They crossed the state line, and 15 minutes later Randy flashed his headlights at Jeff. Jeff pulled the blue Ford over to the roadside, and Randy pulled up behind him. Randy got out of his truck and walked up to Jeff's driver's window. Jeff rolled down the window and said, "What the hell, now? We don't have time for this shit."

"We need to ditch this car!"

"The hell we do! I've got my toy in this trunk."

"Your toy has kicked out one of the taillights. She is the reason we have a dead cop hanging over our heads now."

"We'll get a new set of plates, which should be easy enough," Jeff said. Then he added, "Say, let's pull off on the first secluded road we run across. I have a few things to discuss with our new friend. Just follow me, OK."

Randy nodded and walked back to his truck. After about 10 minutes, Jeff pulled off the highway onto a rutted service road and Randy followed. They drove along in darkness, until they came across a much smaller and less traveled road. Jeff turned off onto that one and they followed it until it ended in a small clearing in the woods.

Jeff got out of the car and opened the trunk. He saw Cindy's cell phone lit up on the floor of trunk. He picked it up, and heard a woman yelling, "Cindy, Cindy, I'm calling the police on our landline. We're going to find you baby!" Jeff's face turned bright red, and he pressed the off button and threw Cindy's phone into the surrounding forest with all his might "You're going to pay for that, you little bitch." He raised his fist up and brought it down hard across her face. "Who the hell were you talking to, Cindy?"

Cindy could taste her own blood in her mouth. She could feel her lips instantly swelling from the force of Jeff's blow and painfully pressing the duct tape harder up against her mouth. She mumbled and whimpered from the pain. He grabbed her by her hair and yanked her out of the trunk and dropped her onto the ground in front of him.

Soon Randy was standing beside him and hissed, "What the hell are you doing now, Jeff?"

"I'm going to give Cindy her first lesson in obedience."

"What's the matter with you? We have to get plates for this car, and get the hell out of here."

"I'll tell you what, Randy, you be a good little brother, and go find me some plates. Cindy and I will be ready to go just as soon as you get back."

Randy looked at the girl lying on the ground. Her eyes were huge and round with fear, as she watched Jeff unbuckling his belt as he sneered down at her. Randy looked at his brother in utter disgust, turned, and did as he was told.

When Sheriff Marker slowed his cruiser, Randy said, "Keep on going. It is a ways down this road." Sheriff Marker accelerated and he turned the heads of a few officers who were huddled in defensive positions next their cars on the roadside. Tension in the car increased with the heavy silence that ensued, until Randy finally said, "Start slowing down, way down." Sheriff Marker did as he was instructed. "Right there, do you see that little rutted road?"

"What road are you talking about?" Sheriff Marker asked.

"That road between that big rock and tree; careful, or you're going to miss the turn." Sheriff Marker did overshoot the turn slightly, so he put his cruiser in reverse. The cruiser behind them did the same.

When the beam from their headlights illuminated the old, narrow, and overgrown road, Sheriff Marker said, "This is what you call a road? I'm not taking my car down that thing."

Chad spoke up and asked, "How far down this path is your fort?"

"It is not far. We parked down this road to hide our truck. We can walk from here."

The other car pulled up behind them and the men got out of their cars. Chad handed Randy a flashlight and said, "OK, Randy, you lead the way."

Randy started up the old logging road, and the other men followed in silence. Chad and Sheriff Marker, both being more seasoned than the two officers from the Elk PD, left their flashlights off. There was no sense in becoming a target, if you didn't need to. Instead, they relied upon the flashlights of the others and light from the moon, when it waxed out from behind brooding clouds. Randy soon trained his light on one side of the road as they walked along. "At last," he said, "Here it is." He held his light steady on a narrow trail, which looked like it had been made by native wildlife. "It is single file for a ways, guys," Randy said, as he started down the path. An owl hooted somewhere deep in the dark forest, alerting his own of the presence of the intruders. It made everyone in their small party tense.

Soon, Randy's chain from the shackles he was wearing got caught on a protruding root, and he fell sprawling to the forest floor, and his flashlight flew out ahead of him and landed in a bush. "Son-of-a-bitch, Randy, I almost wet myself!" Sheriff Marker hissed.

Randy scrambled back to his feet. "I told you guys these shackles were not going to cut it out here, when you put the damn things on me," Randy said. He walked over to a bush and snatched his flashlight. "I'm going to probably break my damn leg while I'm out here tonight. Then you baboons will be sorry, because I'm going to sue the shit out of you."

Sheriff Marker said gruffly, "Randy, just shut the fuck up and get moving." Then the sheriff said, "I'm getting too old for this shit." Chad would have been amused by this small dust-up between these two, if an armed killer wasn't loose in the woods. The use of flashlights had him on edge, but they were necessary, because this forest was dense with undergrowth.

They walked the rest of the way in silence, until the river came into view, when the moon waxed again from behind ever darkening clouds. "It is just over that way," Randy said, shining his flashlight in the direction of the hideout. Two bright flashes came out of the darkness from the general direction of the hideout.

Chad yelled, "Get down!"

Randy yelled, "Jeff, shoot them! There are four of them." Randy was knocked backwards by a bullet. Randy lay upon the ground clenching his stomach with his two hands. "Jeff shot me in the gut! I'm going to die," Randy wailed.

To Chad's disbelief, Sheriff Marker stood frozen like a deer in headlights. The next bullet ripped open his throat, and he fell hard to the ground. One of the officers crawled over to him and clamped his hand over a gaping wound in the sheriff's throat. But, it was to no avail. Sheriff Marker's blood was shooting out between the officer's fingers. The sheriff bled out within minutes.

"Turn off your damn flashlights!" Chad ordered as he returned fire. Then he said to the other two officers, "Cover me!" Both officers returned fire as Chad slipped into the woods.

Chad could hear Randy whimpering, "My big brother shot me. I can't believe he shot me." As Chad closed in on the hideout, he realized the shots were now being fired from the river. Jeff had managed to get the rowboat out into the water, and as Jeff fired at the group the current was carrying his rowboat downstream away from the cabin. Chad returned fire until he realized at this point that pursuing Jeff was of no use. He yelled at the others, "He is on the water. Hold your fire!" Chad then took out his cell phone and called the Elk PD. He said to its commander, "Our suspect is on the river in a rowboat and currently heading downstream back toward your men. Tell them to be on the lookout. And please send a couple of ambulances our way. We have two men shot, one of which is most likely dead by now."

Chad returned to the small group and turned on one of the flashlights to survey the damage done by Jeff. Sheriff Marker's face was a pasty white and a sharp contrast to the crimson ground upon which he lay. Chad gently reached down and closed Sheriff Marker's eyelids. Next, Chad turned and looked at Randy, who was still clenching his gut and moaning. Chad said to the other officers, "I've already called for ambulances, but we need to carry our witness out of here because, I'm afraid if we wait for paramedics to come in here to get him, we could lose our star witness. While I'm here, I'm going to check out this hideout of theirs."

"Sir, if you don't mind me saying, I would have reservations about being out here alone under these circumstances," one of the officers said."

"I'm sure our suspect is long gone. I will be fine, but I understand your concern. After the ambulance picks up Mr. Newton, would you gentlemen direct the coroner's team to Sheriff Marker?"

"Yes, sir, we will."

Chad turned and followed the beam of light from his flashlight in the direction of the hideout. The brush was so overgrown on this part of the riverbank that Chad would have walked right by it, if he had not known it was there. Chad had to part branches with his hands to reach it. He ran his light over the front of the structure. It was squat of stature and made from logs hewn from the surrounding forest, of that Chad was almost certain. It was a relic left over from the beginning of the previous century. Chad made a mental note that its windows had been boarded up. Chad pushed open the door with his flashlight and had to stoop down to enter the doorway. He was able to straighten up once he was through the doorway. He slowly ran his light over the walls of the tiny room. Its windows had wire covering them on the inside, which was bolted from outside. There was also another room, which had an open door with a padlock dangling from its handle. This was the room Chad knew was going to be of most interest to his forensics team. Again, Chad used his flashlight to gently push the open door a bit wider, being careful not to touch anything. He noted a chain was bolted into a wall and on the other end was a small padlock. Chills ran down Chad's spine, and he tried not to imagine the horrors the missing girls endured in their last months, weeks, days, or hours of their lives. Chad knew from his years of experience that the devil truly did walk this earth, and before him was just some of the evidence of the devil's handiwork. This room also had its widows covered in the same manner as the other room. The room reeked of urine. Although Chad didn't want to, he stepped inside the room. There, on the floor near where the chain hung from the wall, with the padlock on its last link, was a recently opened can of chili beans and a nearly empty bottle of water. There was almost nothing missing from the can, which had just started to grow mold. In a corner was a filthy old army blanket. He had not seen one of those in years. It was sure to be a treasure trove of evidence for his forensic team. Chad touched nothing. He walked back into the other room and took a closer look at the few items which were randomly scattered around upon the floor. There was some canned food, crackers, breakfast bars, and bottled water in a backpack. However, Chad found that the most interesting items were in a small unzipped pocket on the backpack. He took a pen from his blazer and used it to spread open the pocket. There inside, were various articles of jewelry. They were mementos from Randy and Jeff's victims, Chad was certain. Next to the jewelry was something that held even more interest for Chad; it was an open bulky envelope of money, a lot of money. Chad ran the tip of his pen over the corner of the bills so he could discern the denomination of the bills. The envelope was stuffed with Benjamin Franklins. Chad guessed this backpack must have been forgotten when Jeff first saw the beam from Randy's flashlight. Chad pulled back the larger opening of the backpack with his pen, and there was a money sack from the robbery, he assumed. The amount of cash in that envelope, Chad knew, was far more than the haul at a convenience store, even in a large city, would take in on any given day. It appeared these brothers had more to tell.

Chad swept the room again with his light, and he let the beam of light come to a rest in the far corner of the room. There on the floor was a small stack of neatly folded papers, which looked odd and out of place considering the haphazard chaos of the rest of that room. Chad walked over and picked up one on top and unfolded it. He got a feeling of his heart dropping in his chest again, when he realized what he was looking at. It was a missing person's poster with a picture of the smiling face of a beautiful brunette. It was the very same poster the older gentleman, who had burst past the line back off highway 9, had shown him of his missing daughter. Chad's memory of the anguished look in the father's eyes made Chad more resolved than ever to find this girl. He didn't touch the other posters, because he wanted to keep this crime scene as pristine as possible, but this poster he took with him as he left the building.

Chad walked back up the trail, and one of the officers had come back with a tarp to cover Sheriff Marker's body, and was watching over it until the coroner's team could arrive. Chad said, "Just down there near the river is an old log cabin. Would you mind taping the perimeter of it off, because the cabin is a crime scene and under no circumstances is anyone to enter, until our forensic team gets here? Is that clearly understood?"

The officer responded, "Yes, sir, I will personally take care of that."

"Thank you. Um, I have one more request."

"What is it, sir?"

"Since I rode here with the sheriff, I need his car keys to get back to Elk." The officer nodded and pulled back the tarp just enough so he could rummage through the sheriff's pockets. Soon, he found what he was looking for, replaced the tarp, and with a grim face handed Chad the keys. "Thank you," Chad said, stepping around Sheriff Marker's body. He proceeded back up the trail to where Sheriff Marker's car was parked. The other officer was there near the cars, so he could show other arriving law enforcement where the trail head was.

Chad said to him, “These woods are dark out here.”

“They are damn creepy, sir.”

“Yeah, an armed killer running around lose, doesn’t help either. But now he knows this place is going to have cops crawling all over it, so you have probably never been safer.”

“I’m sorry about Sheriff Marker, sir”

“I am too, what a damn shame. That guy should have been retired, but I know how that goes,” Chad said.

“Yes, sir, too many of us do. Being married to your job makes for a cold bed.”

“You’re young still. You remember what you just said, and don’t let it happen to you,” Chad said, as he unlocked the cruiser and slid in behind its wheel. He dialed Dan’s number.

Dan picked up the call, “Adams speaking.”

“Dan, this is Turner. I need more hours allocated to Chester’s team. We have another crime scene. Also, I need a cadaver dog team, and a dog water search team, with a diver on board.”

“Placing a marker on the water, if you find something, is not good enough, Chad?”

“We need to know with 100% accuracy if there is a body in that river, or not. Because, if our missing subject is not in the water, we need to keep looking, and as you know time is of the essence. So, no, a marker is not good enough. Also, is everything on track for tomorrow morning?”

“Oh, I was meaning to call you about that.”

“Damn it, Dan, I just hate it when you say that. You know I hate last minute shit!”

"Hey, this is not last minute. You can't say that."

"By your standards, Dan, I will have to concede. What is going on this time?"

"I've got news about your tracker."

"What the hell do you mean; you have news about my tracker?"

"Your team is coming, but they will not be there by 7:00 am."

"Why, are they sleeping in?"

"No, wise guy, I had to pull them from a job on the East Coast. Look, you said you wanted the best in the field, right? I don't have a magic hat that I can pull the best, of the best, out of every time you demand it, you know!"

"Are you saving the best for last, Dan? What time are they going to be here?"

"Their ETA is 11a.m., give or take an hour."

"Well, they will have to meet us on location at that time."

"Where is that going to be?"

"That is yet to be determined. Once we pinpoint it, I will let you know. What about my drone, and sharpshooters?"

"I have been told they will be there at 7 a.m."

"Good deal; I will have my team call you with location coordinates as soon as we have them. Thank you, Dan," Chad said, and ended his call.

It was time for Chad to pay Mrs. Newton another visit and he was hoping that, under the new circumstances, she would be more cooperative. When he pulled into her driveway, the dark surrounding woods and brooding sky made her dilapidated house look like something out of a Steven King movie. And those woods had eyes, this he knew for a fact. He got out of his car and made his way up onto the porch. A chorus of barking dogs sounded on the other side of the door before Chad even knocked. When Chad did knock, it drove the dogs into a barking frenzy and he heard scratching on the other side of the door, and then a dog yelp loudly. Next, he heard someone yell, "Shut your fucking mouths." Then there was another yelp, and he heard, "Who the hell is it?"

"Agent Chad Turner, Mrs. Newton."

She opened the door a crack, while strategically placing a leg in the lower part of its opening to prevent an escape of any of her four legged charges. "What the hell do you want, Mr. FBI man? Don't you know it is late?" she said in a drunken slur. Then she added, "Don't you assholes ever sleep?"

"My apology for such a late hour, Mrs. Newton, but time is of essence."

She cocked one eyebrow at him, and slurred again, "Time is of essence for whom?"

"Time is of essence for all of us, Mrs. Newton."

"Why the hell should I care? Time hasn't meant a damn thing to me for years now."

"Time is of essence for us, because we're trying to bring Jeff in alive, Mrs. Newton."

"You already have Randy. You know he called me wanting an attorney. I don't have any money for an attorney, and I told him so. Now you want me to help you catch my other boy? What the hell do you think I can do?" she said, and started to close the door.

Chad used his foot to block the door from closing and said, "Wait, Mrs. Newton, I am trying to bring Jeff in alive. I would like to think that you would want the same outcome."

She hissed at Chad through bared rotten and stained teeth, "What, so you can kill him later. I'm no damned fool, is that what you take me for, a damned fool?"

"No, Miss Newton, clearly I do not take you for a fool."

"Get the hell off my property, and I hope he shoots you before you and your ilk can kill him."

"I just wanted to ask you a few questions."

"Are you deaf; didn't you hear me? I'm not answering any of your questions, so you're wasting my time and yours."

"As always, Miss Newton, it has been a pleasure," Chad said, and left.

Chapter 11

The following morning Chad stood in front of his new charges in the improvised war room of the Elk PD. He scanned the group of men and women sitting in front of him with a trained eye. It was a fit group of individuals, and the best in their class. Chad said, "When I ask for any given group, of which you're a member, I would like you to rise. When we're done with this exercise, I would like all of you to place your credentials upon this table beside me, before you leave this room. I would like them in team specific piles. I would like to start with our drone operators." Two very young men stood up, who looked to be right out of high school. "Which of you is the commander?"

A red headed young man said, "I am, sir."

"What is your name, please?"

"My name is Greg Cox, sir."

"What kind of UAV are you flying?"

"I'm flying a HLO, with GPS and FLIR, sir."

"Excellent, what is your payload?"

"It is 26 pounds, sir"

"You're the pilot?"

'Yes, I am, sir."

"You will be taking your orders directly from me. Is that understood?"

"Yes, sir, I understand."

Chad looked at the other young man, who was standing next to Greg. "My name is Eddie Dobbs, sir."

"You're the cameraman, I assume?"

"That is correct, sir."

"You may both have a seat."

"Next, let's have our sharpshooters." Six people stood, of which four were men and two were women. Who is the commander of this group?"

A petite brunette woman said, "I am commander, sir. My name is Stella West."

"You will also take your orders directly from me. Is that understood?"

"Yes, sir, I understand."

"Everyone please have a seat." Next, I would like our dog handlers to stand." Sam Duncan and Joe Warren, who had helped Chad find the jeans, stood along with two new additions, which happened to both be women. "I understand your dog's training covers both trail and air scent. Is my understanding correct?"

Joe Warren replied, "Yes, sir, that is correct for my dog. He has been trained to be scent specific, and for hunting hot scent, sir."

"Excellent, please state your name for the rest of our team?" Chad said.

"Joe Warren, sir."

Next, Chad looked at Sam Duncan. "My name is Sam Duncan, and my dog has also been cross trained for both scent specific trailing and hot scent, sir," Sam said.

You will both be taking your orders directly from me. Now you may both be seated."

To the two ladies, who were left standing, Chad said, "You must be our cadaver dog handlers I requested?"

A pretty blonde responded, "Yes, sir, we are."

"Please state you dog's expertise, Miss?"

"I'm Amy Norris, and my dog's expertise is fresh scent, sir, as well as long deceased."

"That is wonderful news, Miss Norris, I'm glad we were able to find you in such a timely manner. I understand that not many dog teams on this side of the country can do both."

"That is true, sir. Thank you for asking us out."

Next, Chad looked at a slender, young woman, with waist length dark brown hair. "What is your dog's expertise, Miss?"

"I'm Trudy Cook, sir. My dog's expertise is cadaver searches and recovery on land and on water."

"Good, then you will be assigned to deploy with our dive team, Miss Cook.

You will both be taking your orders directly from me. Now you may both be seated." Chad then scanned the room and asked, "Where is my dive team?"

A young police officer stepped forward and said, "We just got a call from them a little while back, sir. It seems they are about 20 minutes out."

Chad frowned, and said, "Well, we shall go ahead and proceed without them."

Chad stepped to one side of the room and asked, "Would someone in back dim the lights please?" Next, he pressed a button on a remote he held in his hand, and a larger than life image of Jeff Newton appeared on a projector screen. "This is the subject of our man hunt, and he is armed and dangerous. We have to date, five, and possibly more missing females we believe he and his brother, Randy Don Newton, whom we have in custody, may be responsible for, as well as two dead officers.

Our subject was last seen in a rowboat last night on Badger River, in Badger Creek Wilderness Preserve. He is twenty-four year old

Jeffery Jayson Newton, and he is five feet and eleven inches tall. He has brown hair, hazel eyes, and weighs approximately one hundred and sixty pounds. It is highly desirable to bring him in alive to help with recovery of the victims, if at all possible. If that goal is not attainable, we want him exterminated. Under no circumstances is he to escape capture once we have him located. Is this clearly understood by all of you?"

Chad got a resounding, "Yes, sir," from the small group sitting before him. "Now is the time to ask if anyone has any questions."

The commander of the sharpshooter team raised her hand. "Yes, Miss West," Chad said.

"Does our subject have any prior specialized military training?"

"No, he has never served."

"Thank you, sir."

Just then the dive team entered the room, and a tall, handsome, blonde man said in a deep voice, "Sorry that we're late, sir."

Chad nodded, and said, "You're the diver?"

"Yes, sir, I'm the diver."

Chad motioned with his hand in the direction of Trudy, and said, "Miss Trudy Cook and her scent dog will be teaming up with you and your group. Please state your name for our team?"

"I'm Scott Holder," he said and looked at Trudy with interest. Trudy looked back at him and gave him a shy smile.

Chad asked, "Does everyone have their search coordinates?"

Chad got another resounding, "Yes, sir!"

"Before we deploy, I would like to add that we have an active crime scene out there, which is being processed by our forensic team as we speak. Please be respectful of their tape, and keep the crime scene as uncontaminated as is possible." Chad said, "Now, let's do this!"

The assorted teams piled into their respective vehicles and they all headed out in a caravan toward Badger Creek Wilderness Preserve. As Chad drove along the winding road, he glanced over at Badger River, which ran along the left of the highway. Her banks hugged the rugged mountain, which had long ago lost its peak. Fog lay in thick layers, shrouding her opposite side under a mysterious veil. A cold shiver ran up Chad's spine. Chad had a feeling that mountain was hiding a cold blooded killer. That side of the river was uninhabited for miles. Chad had to resist an urge to start there because, if his years in this field of work had taught him nothing else, the one thing it had taught him was that you never assume anything. Because, when you did, you found out almost immediately you were wrong. Some of his colleagues paid for their mistakes with their lives. He knew this team that he had assembled was a good one. If anyone could find this suspect, they could. And Chester's forensic team was a blessing, because he was damned sure this case was going to stick. All they had to do now was find Cindy, hopefully alive, and catch Jeff, dead or alive, and let the evidence tell the rest of the story about what really went down over the years. He knew that the odds of Cindy still being alive were slim to none.

Ahead of him, Chad saw the vehicle, which was pulling the boat the dive team was using, turn off the road and head toward a boat launch. Trudy, the tall gal, with the long dark hair, followed the boat in her vehicle. Her dog was excitedly hanging out the window, already sniffing the air, eager to get to work. Smiling, Chad wished he lived a life in which he too could have a dog, but only for a split second, because he knew that would never be for him. The rest of the caravan continued on toward the hideout. Dotted along the roadway were police vehicles of various makes and models. The search for Jeff was still in full swing. Soon the caravan reached its destination. As the team walked the trail toward the hideout, Amy's black Labrador Retriever alerted on the taped off section of the trail where Sheriff Marker had fallen. Amy rewarded her dog with a treat and took the dog off his leash. The dog wagged his whole body in excitement and put his nose to the ground and got to work. Amy quietly followed along behind her dog. The sharpshooters took positions strategically around the perimeter of the property of the hideout, scanning the woods for any sign of movement with trained eyes.

Chad stepped underneath the yellow ribbon that taped off the hideout from the rest of the crime scene. When Chad ducked into the small cabin, he was surprised how vastly different it looked under the harsh glare of the battery operated lights which illuminated the first room and also the room behind the single interior door. Chad nodded to some of Chester's crew that was working in the first room, then he stepped through the interior door and found Chester crouched over the roughly hewn floor planks. He was closely examining them, and carefully bagging some evidence into separate bags.

Chester looked up as Chad stepped into the room. "Did you sleep in?" Chester asked.

"No, wise guy, I did not sleep in. I just thought it would be polite to wait for the rest of my team, so I could brief them on what our goals and objectives will be out here today. What have you got there?"

"Hair; red hair, blonde hair, brown hair, black hair and a molar, you name it."

"Could some of the hair be from our suspects?"

"Most of the hair that I'm finding is long, with roots intact, and there is some with bits of scalp, I'm afraid to say."

Chad frowned, and said, "Those dark spots all over the walls look like blood splatter to me."

Chester nodded, and said, "Yes, the floorboards have been soaked in blood in places." Chester stood up, stretched, and yawned. "This is going to be a long day."

"Have you had any sleep?"

"Since yesterday, negative, they called me in late last night, but hey, I'm going to get a second wind any moment now. Did you see the pile of posters bagged up in the other room?"

"I saw them yesterday, and I took the one on the top, but I didn't touch the other ones. I didn't want to contaminate the scene."

"That consideration is always appreciated, by the folks in my field. The hair I'm finding in here appears to be a pretty close match to those girls in the posters, even without further analyses, that is except for this long black hair. It seems that your perpetrators have an affinity for trophies, judging by the posters, and the random jewelry which we found in a backpack. They also left behind $10,000 in the same backpack. It appears they left in a real hurry."

Chad said, "Yeah, you could say they did, since we already have one of them. The million dollar question is, where did that 10 Gs come from, and why, and whom does the long black hair belong to?" Just then, Chad's cell phone rang, "Turner, here."

"Sir, this is Amy. My dog has a hit."

"What's your location, Amy, in relation to the cabin?"

"We're about 400 yards and almost directly behind the cabin, sir."

"Stay there, I'm on my way."

Chester looked at him, "Good news?"

"Probably not for one of those girl's family members, but one of the cadaver dog teams has a hit about 400 yards behind this cabin. I'm going to go check it out right now. I'll see you in a bit. Hey, is this cabin to the point yet where we can bring in that dog?"

"Now would be perfect timing."

"OK, we will see you in just a few," Chad said, and made his way out of the cabin in search of Amy and her canine. On his way to find Amy, Chad placed a call to Dan.

"Hello, Adams, speaking."

"Dan, this is Chad, could you get us a forensic excavation team out here to assist Chester's team, ASAP?"

"Well certainly, is there anything else I can be of help with for you Chad? Maybe I can send you unicorns or perhaps a Pegasus?"

"Well, now that you mention it, Dan, where the hell is my tracker?"

"She is on her way, and should be there momentarily. Enjoy your hunt, and keep your head down."

"Thank you for your sentiments, Dan," Chad said sarcastically, and ended the call.

Chad approached Amy and her dog. The dog was lying at her feet, wagging his tail, and happily chewing on a toy. "Well, Amy, this is a job well done, and a good start. Could you please have one of the officers mark this location for you. Also, Chester, who is the head of the forensic team, is waiting for you two down at the cabin. Would you mind doing a sweep of the inside?"

"Certainly, sir, we are on our way," she said, and reached down and took the toy away from the dog, much to the dog's dismay.

Chads cell phone rang again, "Turner, here."

"Agent Turner, this is Greg Cox, the drone commander."

"Go ahead, Greg, what do you have?"

"We have located the rowboat, sir."

"How are you sure that is the rowboat we're searching for?"

"This particular rowboat has more than just a few bullet holes in it, sir."

Chad felt a smile spread across his face. Now they had a known starting point for a hot scent search. What is your location, Greg?"

"My location is about a mile south of the cabin. But, sir, the rowboat is on the other side of the river from us. Sir, I just spied a huge predator coming in."

"What did you just say?"

"Sorry, sir, that is our team's lingo for a helicopter, it's coming your way now, sir."

"OK, thank you, and would you please contact the others and have everyone who was at the meeting this morning meet up at the boat launch area, except the cadaver teams?"

"Will do, sir," Greg said, and ended the call.

As Chad walked out of the woods to the road, he called the local Sheriff's office and asked that they bring their water craft, which was out on the river for the search, back to the launch area. He explained that his crew needed a lift across the river. Chad was just finishing up his call as his voice was being drowned out by the sound coming from the powerful rotors on the helicopter, as it was hovering just above him, preparing to set down. The branches on the trees that surrounded the area bent backwards under the force of the wind, which came from the powerful blades. The helicopter rocked momentarily just above the ground before it set down. One woman and two men emerged from the helicopter. The pilot handed down duffle bags and other items to the three on the ground. As the pilot prepared to take the helicopter back up, the three new arrivals jogged toward Chad. As they stood beside Chad, they turned and watched the helicopter take back to the sky, while Chad looked at this latest addition to his group. He could not take his eyes off of this woman. She was gorgeous; there was just no other way to describe her. Her long auburn hair swirled all around her, catching the rays of sunlight, and casting out flashes here and there, which looked like fire. Then there was the way she filled out the jumpsuit she was wearing. Every curve was in just the right proportion to the other curves; Chad knew he was in trouble.

She looked at him with her hazel eyes, smiled brightly at him, and extended her hand to him. He didn't know if he dared to touch her. He had never felt so dumbfounded in his entire life. It felt to him like he was moving in slow motion, as he reached his hand out and touched her. There was an electric charge that tingled up his arm and elsewhere too. He knew he needed to get a grip on this feeling; he needed to handle this. Then he thought, no that was the wrong damn phrase, because exactly what he wanted to do was handle it, this gorgeous creature, which was standing in front of him. This was running through his mind at lightning speed, as he shook her hand, and said over the sound of the receding helicopter, "Chad Turner, FBI Special Task Force Commander."

"Running Fawn O'Brian, my friends simply call me Fawn. I am very pleased to meet you, Commander."

A man about 38, Chad's age, held out his hand to Chad, "Barnard Haddix, sir,"

"Nice to meet you, Barnard, welcome to our team."

"Thank you, sir.

A young, skinny guy stepped forward and held out a surprisingly large hand to Chad, "Mikey Noonan, at your service, sir."

Chad held his hand out to Mikey and in amazement watched it nearly disappear when Mikey closed his hand around Chad's, as the two men shook hands.

Chad said, "I wish I could offer the three of you each a nice room to rest and freshen up, because I know you've had a long trip, but we have one hell of a bad ass loose on the other side of this river that needs to be apprehended. Are the three of you ready to get to work?"

All three of the new arrivals said in unison, "Yes, sir!"

"OK, then we have a boat waiting for us. The three of you can ride with me. My car is this way," Chad said, as he reached for Fawn's heavy duffel bag, which she let him take. As Chad swung it over his shoulder, Mikey looked at Barnard and winked. Barnard smiled back at Mikey knowingly. Fawn caught their silent exchange, rolled her eyes, shook her head, and fell into step behind Chad.

Sam and his bloodhound were already aboard the boat that was waiting for Chad and his party. As they were boarding one of the boats, Chad felt a light wind starting to come up off the water. He was hoping the wind wouldn't get any stronger, because it could make tracking a hot scent more difficult for the dogs. As they were motoring across the river, Chad asked Fawn, "How did you get into this line of work?"

"As a little girl, my Grandfather, who is from the Choctaw Nation, used to take me hunting with him. We would track an animal, sometimes for miles. The tracks and other signs along the way always fascinated me, and," she shrugged prettily, "I just never out grew my fascination of it, so here I sit."

Chad smiled at her, "He didn't have any grandsons?"

"Oh, he did, but after a while the boys lost interest. They would rather play their video games than go out into the wilderness with Gramps. So he taught me everything he knew, and that knowledge was passed down to him from the generations who came before us."

"There aren't very many of you left who can track like that anymore, is there?"

"No, there aren't, which is a pity, isn't it? But, how did you know that?"

"The Bureau makes it their job to know helpful information like this."

"Yes, I suppose they would need to."

Chad could now make out the rowboat, which was partially dragged up on the bank of a marshy part of the river, in an attempt to obscure it from view. Chad pointed toward the rowboat, which was indeed riddled with bullet holes. "It looks like this will be a good starting point for us." Chad saw that the octocopter was buzzing up and down the shoreline on that side of the river, and then it cut inland, until it was out of sight. Chad knew it was a great resource to have, because it could cover miles in a short period of time. The dive team, with Trudy and her dog, had picked up Joe and his dog and were just dropping them off along with Stella and the other female sharpshooter, when the boat with Chad and the others pulled up. Stella smiled warmly at Fawn and the others, and said, "I would like to introduce you to Cara; she is the go to if anything happens to me." A tall slender Asian woman smiled sweetly and shook everyone's hands as she was introduced to them.

Joe walked up to them with his young dog, which playfully bounded toward Sam's bloodhound. Chad looked at Fawn and asked, "How would you like us to proceed with this tracking?"

Fawn reached her hand out to Joe, "I'm Fawn, and I'm very pleased to have the pleasure to work with you, Joe. These two gentlemen are my assistants, Barnard and Mikey." The two men shook Joe's hand. Then, Fawn turned toward Chad. "It has been my experience that it yields the best results to allow Joe and his canine to work the hot scent for as long as he can. When that trail grows cold, that is where my team and I come into play. As he already knows, he can still continue to try to pick up the hot scent again or possibly pick it up again when my team and I find a sign of his trail. When I work alongside a dog handler, I have found that we're able to clear vastly larger tracts of land than either of us working independently of each other would ever be able to accomplish."

Chad said, "Gentlemen, you heard the lady, we now have a plan, go ahead and execute." Chad looked from the shore of the river out over the heavily forested mountain, which loomed up before him. The scope of the daunting task, which lay before them, was not lost on him. Chad could see the drone zigzagging back and forth around the tops of the towering pine trees, which heavily clad the mountain side. He turned and faced the Badger River again, and scanned it with his eyes. He could see the dive team's boat methodically going back and forth on the water. Trudy's Springer Spaniel was crouched low on the bow of the bass boat. The dog's nose was almost touching the water. Chad walked over and looked at the rowboat, and there on one of the seats was blood, not much, but it was there, and it was reasonably fresh. The question was, did the blood belong to Jeff or did it belong to Cindy Porter? Chad intended to find out. He took his cell phone out of his pocket and called Dan.

"Hello, Adams, speaking."

"Dan, this is Turner. Could you add a few more hours to Chester's forensic team? We have another potential crime scene out here."

"I've got an idea, Chad, why the hell don't we just put them on the damn payroll as full time employees?"

"As always, it has been a pleasure speaking with you, Dan," Chad said, and ended the call while Dan was still ranting on. Chad didn't have time, nor was he in any mood, for Dan's usual stream of shit. Chad called Chester.

"Hello?"

"Chester, this is Turner. Do you have someone whom you can send over on this side of the river? We have a rowboat over here with blood in it. We were told by the suspect, whom we have in custody, Cindy Porter was last seen diving into the river from this rowboat, and this could be her blood, if she was shot. Or, we could have a wounded suspect; in either case; we need to know who this blood belongs to. Also, could your lab put a rush on it?"

"It'll cost you another beer."

"Deal," Chad started to end the call when Chester spoke again, "Chad, Amy and her dog found another girl buried out here. She is the girl whom you took the poster of."

"How do you know, she has been gone for three years?"

"Well, I'm going on an assumption, because she had on a dress which fits the description of the dress the girl had been wearing when she went missing. Anyway, it looks like it was the dress from what I can ascertain from what is left of it anyway."

"She was in a shallow grave?"

"It was a few feet down, but it has been rutted up by wild hogs and scattered to kingdom come. The scattered bones have Amy's dog in fits. The recovery of any other girls is going to be much more difficult, if they are buried in the immediate vicinity."

Chad had the sinking feeling in his gut again, as he swallowed hard and thought about the girl's father, who had approached him while Chad was dealing with the reporters, and said, "Chester, try to keep the part about the hogs under wraps, if you can. Her family doesn't need to know that."

"I completely understand, Chad. But because of the situation, this job is going to take many man hours. I just thought it was prudent to give you a heads up."

"Every job has its own unique set of challenges, Chester."

"In my line of work, don't I know? Look, I will have one of my technicians come over there and take care of the rowboat for you ASAP. I'll talk to you soon, buddy."

"Thank you, Chester," Chad said, and ended the call.

Chad looked over as the two dog teams worked down the bank of the river. He followed along behind them, and both dogs seemed to be pretty excited. They were moving along at a pretty good clip, when suddenly, the dogs stopped and acted like they wanted to go in the water. Chad shook his head and thought that is one of the oldest tricks there is, when someone takes to the water while trying to throw the dogs off the scent. Chad saw Fawn walking up ahead of the dog teams. She was scouring the wet bank with her well trained eyes. Chad saw Fawn stop and kneel down on the bank. She looked like she was intently studying something there. She looked up and saw Chad was watching her, so she motioned for him to come to her. Chad quickened his pace because he was surprised at this point that she was motioning for him and not the dog teams, which she was working with. By the time Chad reached Fawn, her two assistants were also studying the ground beside her.

Fawn looked up at Chad and said, "It appears that we have company."

Chad said, "What are you talking about?" Chad looked at the river bank in front of them. There on the bank, just out of reach of the gently slapping waves, was a footprint. You could see the toes and everything clearly in the sandy mud. The footprint was small like it was made by a child or a woman, and certainly not by someone the size of Jeff. A blue jay let out an alarming scream and they all jumped, because their nerves were all on edge. Chad said, "My God, she is out here somewhere with him."

Fawn said, "Negative, she is not with him. At least she wasn't when she left this imprint."

Chad looked back down the river bank and saw Sam and Joe were headed toward them; once again the dogs had picked back up the scent. Chad walked toward them quickly. When he met up with the two dog handlers, he asked, "I know this is a long shot, but do either one of you have Cindy Porter's scent items with you?"

Joe said, "I have the bag in the trunk of my car on the other side of the river, sir."

"Excellent," Chad said. He then called the local sheriff's office and asked if they could send a boat back over to them. Chad saw one of the boats turn on the water and head back toward them right after he made his call. When the young deputy pulled his water craft up to the shoreline, Chad explained the situation to him, and Chad asked if the deputy could retrieve the item from Joe's trunk for them. The deputy agreed and Joe handed him the key. Chad then turned to Joe and said, "When he gets back with the scent article, I want you to split off from this group and track Cindy, if in fact that is really a print from her, and it may be. I will send two of the sharpshooters with you for cover while you search."

Joe looked over at the sharpshooters, who had strategically taken positions up and down the river bank, smiled and said, "I'll take the two good looking ones."

Chad smiled and responded, "You need to stay focused, so therefore I'll let you have one of them, is that fair enough."

"OK, I'll take the little brunette."

"No, she stays with me."

Joe faked a frown, and said, "OK, if that is the best I can get, I'll take it."

"I could let you have two of the guys?"

"No, no, I'm a happy man."

"OK, that is more like it. I like to keep the members of my team's morale up," Chad said, smiling as he turned and walked back to where Fawn was working.

When Chad returned, Fawn and her team, along with Sam and his dog, were working farther up the riverbank. It appeared that their suspect was making his way back in the direction of the hideout. It made sense to Chad that the suspect would go to the area in which he was the most familiar. Chad saw Sam working his dog back and forth along the water's edge. Sam looked up at Chad, frowned, and said, "We've lost the damn scent. It looks like he went for a good swim to throw us off track."

Chad looked over at Fawn, who was slightly up the riverbank from them. She was closely examining a tree, which partially hung over the water. Chad walked up to her. She looked at him and pointed a long, slim finger at a branch which protruded out over the water. Fawn said to Chad, "That bough has a partial break, which is fresh, where it branches from the trunk." She walked to another tree which stood right next to it. She tilted her head back and gazed up into the tree, exposing her long slender neck. Chad had to fight to stay focused and when he pulled his gaze away from her lovely throat, she was watching him from the corner of her eye. He was clearly busted. She walked up to the tree and climbed up onto a few of its branches. She looked down at Chad and said, "The bark is scuffed up." She looked around her and stepped from a branch of that tree to the branch of yet another tree, and on to the next without ever touching the ground. Then she jumped back down onto the ground and surveyed the nearby trees to determine which lofty course the suspect had most likely taken. She said to the group around her, "He has come out of the water by way of this low hanging branch and has taken to the trees to try to throw us off his track. I can pretty much tell which trees he used. What we need to carefully look for is where he came down, so we can start the ground tracking again, because when he is in these trees with this wind whipping up, it scatters the scent too much for the hounds." The group followed Fawn, with the four other sharpshooters positioning themselves in a protective semicircle around them. They came to the water's edge again, and Fawn stepped back up into another tree, which also partially hung out over the water. She looked down at them and said, "He is back in the water again."

Barnard said, "He is one smart bastard, isn't he?"

Fawn looked down at her tracking partner, smiled and said, "Did I ever tell you how much I love a good challenge?"

Chad spoke up and said, "Well, from his trajectory so far, it might be a safe bet to assume he is going back in the direction of his cabin, because he would know the wooded area directly across from it better than any of this down here."

"Who knows what goes through the mind of a desperate madman?" Sam said, as he let his dog drink from the river.

Fawn said, "The good news is that he would be swimming upstream against the current. My guess is that he would be sticking close to the bank and using whatever vegetation he could to pull himself along, wherever he can."

Sam said, "I got you, let's move."

It was always fascinating to watch how these tracking teams worked together, Chad thought, as he walked slowly along the riverbank with them as they methodically did their work. Chad was not surprised when Fawn's deduction of the situation proved to be spot on the mark. Sam's dog, while working the river's edge, would hit on the scent only to quickly lose it again. Chad called Joe to see how his search for Cindy, if that imprint did indeed belong to her, was coming along.

Joe answered, after a few rings. "Hello, this is Joe."

"Joe, this is Turner. How is it looking? Is it her?"

"Affirmative, we have a scent!"

Chad's mood was buoyed. "That is wonderful news. What Randy said was true. She is still alive, but now all we have to do is find her, before Jeff does. Stay in close touch with us Joe."

"I sure will."

"Thank you, Joe," Chad said, ending the call. Chad made another call to the dive team, and said, "Our subject is alive, and we're searching for her now."

The voice on the other end said, "That is awesome news, Commander! We will wrap this up."

"Would you mind passing the phone to Trudy, please?"

"Hold on, sir, just a second."

There was a slight pause before Trudy's voice came on the phone. "Hello, this is Trudy speaking."

"Hello, Trudy, would you please return to the cabin and help Amy with the search of the area surrounding the cabin?"

"Yes, I certainly will. And that is wonderful news about the missing girl, Agent Turner."

"She is still missing. Hopefully, we will find her in time."

"Godspeed to you and your crew over there," Trudy said.

"Thank you, Trudy." Chad returned his focus to the matter of finding Jeff.

Chad looked around, and everyone, who was within hearing range of his phone conversations, was smiling. It was a good feeling to see so many happy faces. He had to fight off the strong urge to call the local sheriff to have them notify Mr. and Mrs. Porter that their daughter was still alive. Chad knew, however, in this line of work, things could go to hell in a hand basket quicker than you could blink an eye. "Let's get back at it."

About 30 minutes later, Sam's bloodhound was able to pick up the scent of Jeff again. The hound started to track inland again. With his tail wagging and his nose to the ground, the dog was clearly excited, and the feeling of excitement spread to his human companions. There were a few times Jeff had taken to the trees again, but now those Tarzan style adventures were short lived. Chad was pretty certain it was because Jeff was wearing down. An hour later and once more it appeared that Jeff had taken to the trees, and the bloodhound had lost the scent, because it had scattered too much on the wind.

While Fawn and her team were searching for clues as to where he might have come down, she ran cross a large clump of wild berries there in a sunny clearing. She searched around the clump for any sign of Jeff and what she found made her blood run cold. There, sparkling in the sunlight, and dangling off a berry branch like a golden icicle, was a few strands of long blonde hair. What were the odds of those two crossing each other's paths again on a mountain of this size? Fawn was just raising her hand to point this new find out, when the sound of a single gunshot reverberated off the mountainside. All heads turned in the direction of the gunfire, which came from a rocky outcrop high above them. Only one shot had been fired, and Chad knew his drone operators were up there. He furrowed his brows and made a call to the drone commander, Greg Cox.

"Hello, Greg, speaking."

"Greg, this is Turner. It sounds like you might have some company up there?"

"Yes, sir, I was just fixing to call you about that. Your suspect just tried to take down my drone. It received some damage, but we're still in the air."

"Greg, you guys stay close to those two sharpshooters. You two guys are sitting ducks without them."

"We're trailing them as we speak, Commander. We're all climbing up the mountain after the suspect."

"Try to hold off, until we can reach you. Try not to push him too hard."

"No can do, sir, he is on the move. We need to stay on top of him, or we're going to lose him again. These thick pine trees make for poor visibility on the ground for the drone. But you're the commander, so you call the shots."

Chad frowned, "Stay on him, but hang back until we can get there. Greg, I don't need to tell you he is one badass. I'm just concerned for the safety of my team."

"I understand, Commander, and I appreciate you factoring in our safety. We will keep our heads low."

"Greg, there is one more thing."

"What is it, Commander?"

"We have confirmed Cindy Porter is on this mountain as well."

Just when Chad made that statement, Fawn motioned frantically to get Chad's attention, while he was still on the call with Greg. "Wait, Greg, hold on for just a moment. It appears something has come up."

Chad walked over to the blackberry bush where Fawn was standing. Fawn pointed to the few strands of long blonde hair, which at first Chad did not see. "I'll be damned, Fawn, you're good. How the hell did you find this?"

"She is here, sir. We have got to find her."

Chad nodded in reply, and put the phone back up to his ear. "Greg, we're going to send a hound team and one more sharpshooter up your way. We're splitting our group up. Stella and I will accompany Fawn and her team to track the girl; because she is close, very close it appears. Keep your eye in the sky on the lookout for her."

"We will Commander, and the best of luck to you, your crew with you, and of course, the girl. See you soon."

Chad turned and called out to Stella, the commander of the sharpshooters. She turned her attention from guarding their perimeter and, with the nose her M24 SWS pointed at the ground, approached Chad. Her soft brown eyes looked up at him from underneath long, lush eyelashes. "Yes, Commander, what is it?"

"We're splitting off. You're staying with Fawn, her team and myself to search for Cindy, because she is somewhere nearby us right now. The dog team and your other shooter will go continue the search for Jeff. I can't risk him finding her before we do."

Stella nodded, knowingly, "That is understood, sir. I will go let him know that he is going with Sam and his dog."

Chad said, "OK, folks, let's push this as hard and fast as we can. We're approaching a critical point. Let's move out!"

Fawns two assistants flanked her on either side holding their lights oblique to the ground, helping her search for any indication of even the slightest disturbance of the forested floor of the mountainside. Fawn picked up a snapped twig and examined it closely. She smiled and said, "This is fresh." She then pointed and said, "She is tracking this way." They followed a narrow, meandering, trail made by wildlife. A large screeching hawk flew out of a tree just over their heads, startling them. Stella brought her M24 SWS up, tucked the butt deep into her shoulder, set her legs, and swept the immediate area with the lethal nose of the barrel. Chad had his pistol gripped in both hands, when he looked at her and nodded. Relieved, she smiled and nodded back, and they both relaxed their hold on their weapons. They were all on edge and their nerves were raw. Chad was very glad to have her on his team.

Stella took up the rear, but her attention was primarily focused ahead and to the sides of them. From the rear position, she was better positioned to respond with her weapon, because she had to ensure the safety of Fawn and Fawn's two assistants. Chad was the only other one with weapons, and he was directly behind Fawn and the other two men with Fawn. When the hawk had taken wing, it had set off alarm bells. Wildlife was one of the best indicators that something in the forest was amiss. In this case the hawk was alerting on them.

In the meantime, Joe was still tracking Cindy with his dog and was following a wildlife trail, which ran along a ridge of the mountain, while the two sharpshooters with him scoured the surrounding area. Joe and his team had almost caught up to where Chad was with his group when another shot rang out from the mountain above him. Joe's beloved hound yelped in pain over and over again. Joe instinctively grabbed his dog and dove for cover, just as another shot hit a rock where Joe had been standing and ricocheted off, with a distinctive ping. Joe's two lethal companions immediately returned fire.

Chad and his group heard the gunfire and the dog yelping just up ahead. Stella sprang into action, sending a volley of bullets up the mountain toward where the fire had come from. She knew it was risky, because they did not know Cindy's location yet, but she also knew her fire could provide her comrades cover so they could seek protective shelter. They all ran in the direction of the yelping dog. The two sharpshooters, who were with Joe when his dog was shot, radioed Stella that they were making their way up the hill. She in turn radioed the rest of her team to hold their fire, unless fired upon. She looked at Chad and he nodded. "Thank you, commander," she said, and then she radioed her crew to tell them she was also on her way up toward where the gunfire had originated from.

Chad and Fawn rounded a bend on the trail and saw Joe huddled with his young hound. Joe was covered in blood and tears were streaming down his face. Fawn kneeled down beside him, and Chad asked him, "Have you been hit?" Joe's lower lip quivered as he looked down at his dog in his lap and he simply shook his head, because he couldn't speak.

Fawn slipped the straps of her jumpsuit off her shoulders and took off her blouse, and with her teeth ripped the blouse into wide strips. She said, "Joe, hold his head firmly." Joe did as he was asked, and a glimmer of hope lit up in Joe's eyes, and in amazement he watched this beautiful woman, as she set out to save his beloved dog's life. First she made a tourniquet out of one of the shreds from the blouse. The bullet had torn into the hound's lower thigh. Next, she looked at Chad, and said, "Commander, please help hold this dog still, because this is going to be painful for him." Chad did as he was asked. Fawn packed the gaping wound with more of the material and tied the one remaining shred of materiel to hold the packing in place. The packing quickly soaked up the blood of the hound, so she tied it a little tighter. Sam doubled back at the sound of the yelping dog, and came around the corner with his hound and the sharpshooter Chad had sent with him. Sam's eyes teared up at the sight before him, as he held his dog back. Fawn looked up at the sharpshooter, and asked, "Do you have a bag?"

"Do you mean a body bag?"

"Yes, and does anyone have a knife?"

"I have one," Sam said, digging into his backpack and handing it to Fawn.

When the sharpshooter handed her a body bag, she took the knife and cut a hole into each corner, and then she walked over and picked up a fallen tree limb and tested it for strength. She used the heel of her boot to shave off as many of the branches as she could, and then she used the knife to whittle off the rest. She looked around for another branch she could use. Soon she found one but, when she applied the heel of her boot, she was met with more resistance, because this one had fallen from the tree more recently.

Chad walked over to her, and said, "Here let me give you a hand with that?" Just then another shot rang out, and Chad wrapped his arms around her and pulled her down onto the ground with him. The single shot was answered with a volley of return fire from the sharpshooters. Chad could feel her soft, ample, breast pressed against his chest, and the sweet scent of her breath wafted up at him, luring him. Reluctantly, he pulled away from her, and said to everyone, "We all need to stay low." Chad pulled the branch with him as he followed Fawn back over to where the others were. Once there, Chad pulled out a huge hunting knife and made short work of the resistant growth on the limb. When he was done, he handed it to Fawn. When their eyes met, he could have been mistaken, but he could almost swear he saw a new spark in her eyes, and it felt like his heart flipped in his chest.

"Thank you," she said. The men watched her as she slipped one of the tree limbs into one hole at the top of the body bag and out the other hole. Then she did the same thing on the bottom end. She then looked at Chad and said, "Commander, Joe is going to need someone to help him carry his dog out. I am willing to give up one of my assistants."

Chad looked at Joe, who looked back at him with hopeful and pleading eyes. Then to the sharpshooter Chad said, "You go with them, to cover them. I'll cover us here."

"Yes, sir," the sharpshooter said.

Joe lovingly placed his dog down on the improvised stretcher, and then crouching low he went to Fawn, embraced her and planted a kiss on her cheek. Then he pulled back from her and said, "I will forever be grateful for this. Thank you, Fawn."

Softly she said to him, "Keep us posted, you shall both be in my prayers. Now go with Godspeed."

Chad said to Sam, "Joe was the intended target and now you will be, because he wants to get these dogs off his trail, so keep down as much as you can, Sam."

Sam looked at Chad and narrowed his eyes, "I'm going to get that bastard, sir."

"Don't be a hero, Sam. We need both you and Fawn right now. With these pine trees, the drone is of almost no use, other than to keep Jeff on the move to wear him down."

"I understand, sir." Sam then turned to his assigned sharpshooter and said, "Let's go get him." With the hound leading the way, the two men cautiously began to ascend the mountain.

Fawn then turned to her two assistants and said, "Which one of you would like to help Joe take his hound down?

Then Barnard, the older of the two said, "I will stay with you, because Mikey has little ones at home."

Fawn looked at the younger man and Mikey nodded his head and said, "I'll go."

"Thank you. We will see you when we get back," Fawn said.

Chad called Stella, and said, "We need some cover fire, because Joe is taking his wounded hound down on a stretcher."

"Roger that, Commander," Stella said. A few seconds later gunfire erupted on the mountain above them.

Chad told Joe, "That's your cover, go."

Joe and the other man picked up the stretcher, and headed back down the mountain with their sharpshooter taking up the rear, while keeping an eye on the mountain above him.

Chad looked at Fawn and asked her, "Are you ready?"

"I've been ready, sir."

Chad followed Fawn and her one remaining assistant as they began tracking Cindy again. He had his .40 caliber Glock in his hand and his high powered rifle on his shoulder.

Cindy's path continued to follow the path made by the wildlife of the mountainside, which in all her years of tracking made perfect sense to Fawn. Fawn said, "She is following this animal path, and that is how she found the berries. That makes sense to me, but something frightened her away from the food source."

Chad looked at the wilderness path in front of them and frowned, because it was heading up the mountain where Jeff was. The terrain was beginning to grow rocky and the pine trees were less dense at this elevation, as they continued their ascent. The drone was zigzagging back and forth almost directly overhead, which concerned Chad, so he called Greg.

Greg picked up on the second ring, "Yes commander, what is it?"

"Do you still have the subject in sight?"

"Affirmative, sir, we have him in sight off and on, because he is trying to use the pine canopy to throw us off his trail."

"Your drone is almost right over us. Keep an eye out for the girl. We have to take defensive action. Let me know as soon as anything changes," Chad said.

Next, Chad called Stella, "Stella speaking."

"Stella, this is Turner. Fawn and her assistant are here with me, and we're all almost directly underneath the drone."

"I will alert my team. Sir, we're all heading your way."

"Thank you, Stella." Chad just ended the call, when he saw something move in the bushes up ahead of him. He raised his gun and took aim. Cindy came darting out of the bushes, looked at him pointing the gun at her, and ran in a blind panic away from him. Chad started after her, when Fawn said, "Commander, stand down! Let me go after her." Without waiting for a response from Chad, Fawn took off down the trail after Cindy.

Cindy dove back into the bushes, and just when Fawn was going to go in after her Jeff stepped out from behind a tree and pointed his gun squarely at Fawn's chest.

"Well, will you look at what I have here," Jeff said, as he leered at Fawn, and she felt her skin crawl under his gaze. Suddenly, Jeff heard movement in the bushes. He trained his gun on the bushes and said, "Come on out and join the party, Cindy hot-stuff."

Fawn started to move, so Jeff trained the gun barrel back on her and said, "I wouldn't do that, if I were you." Then Jeff walked over to Fawn and grabbed her by the hair and pulled her toward the bushes where Cindy was crouching, frozen by fear. Jeff screamed at Cindy, "I said, come out and join the party, Cindy hot-stuff. Are you fucking deaf?" Then, Jeff fired into the bushes where Cindy was hiding.

Chad heard Cindy scream, so he called Greg. Greg answered the phone on the first ring. "Yes, commander, this is Greg."

As Chad was coming around a bend in the trail, Chad told Greg, "Crash into that bastard!" Chad then came into full view of Jeff and trained his weapon on Jeff.

Just then Stella stepped boldly from out of the bushes with the laser of her M24 SWS homed in on Jeff's chest. Jeff nervously waved his gun back and forth pointing it first at Chad and then at Stella.

Overhead the drone went into a dive, and another sharpshooter stepped out of the bushes. Jeff yanked Fawn closer to his body and was bringing his weapon up to her head, when she yanked away, just as the drone crashed into Jeff's throat. Stella was just about to squeeze the trigger on her M24 SWS when she saw Cindy rise up out of the bushes. With surprising strength and agility, Cindy swung a tree limb like a baseball bat and struck Jeff across the face with it, driving the cartilage of his nose into his brain, killing him instantly. One of Stella's sharpshooters knelled down next to where Jeff had fallen, checked his pulse and held up a triumphant fist into the air.

A wicked smile spread across Stella's lips as she gave the order, "Bag it!"

Chad looked over at Cindy as she stood sobbing and broken on the trail. He watched as Fawn slowly approached her and gently took Cindy into her arms. Cindy laid her head on Fawns shoulder as loud sobs shook Cindy's body.

Fawn smoothed Cindy's hair back and cooed to her softly, "There, it is all over now. You are safe. We're taking you home!"

Chad called the Elk police chief and said, "Chief, this is Turner, we need a medevac on the mountain."

"Congratulations, Turner, you got your suspect?"

"We got him sir, but the medevac is for the Porter girl."

"Oh my God, you were able to find her alive?"

Chad was in no mood to go into details on the phone, so he cut the conversation short, "I will have the coordinates sent to you right away, sir," Chad said abruptly, ending the call.

Chad looked over at Cindy, who was sitting upon the ground, leaning against Fawn, as Stella approached her with a bottle of water. Cindy took the water from Stella and greedily turned the bottle up to her lips with trembling hands. Stella was joined by the other female sharpshooter, Cara, and together they laid their weapons upon the ground and sat down in a tight circle in front of Cindy and Fawn. Chad watched as Cara said something to Cindy, and after Cindy finished her water, she cupped her hands as Cara poured water from a bottle into Cindy's palms, and Cindy splashed the cool water upon her swollen and battered face.

Greg and Eddie stepped out of the woods and walked over to where Jeff had crumpled upon the ground, still clinching some of Fawn's long red hair in his fist. Together the two men inspected their busted-up machine, which had Jeff's blood all over it. Eddie looked over at Chad, smiled, and said, "Dan is going to be pissed."

"Yeah, he is going to have our heads on a platter for this," Greg said.

Chad saw Fawn getting up from the ground where she had been sitting with Cindy, and the other two women scooted next to Cindy, until they were flanking her. Fawn approached Greg and Eddie, and said, "I want to thank you two for saving my life."

Eddie smiled shyly at her and said, "As much as we would love to take credit for that, Fawn, the commander saved your life."

Fawn turned her gaze toward Chad. She made eye contact with him and held it, as she slowly approached him. She extended her slender hand to him and he lightly took her hand in his. There were those electrical tingles up his arm again, and the rest of his body responded. And yes, he could see a distinctive light flicker in her eyes, as she said, "Thank you for saving my life, Commander."

"They saved your life, Fawn."

"We were just following orders. It was the Commander's quick thinking, Fawn, which saved not only you, but Cindy as well," Greg said.

Fawn gave Chad's hand an affectionate squeeze and said, "It has been an incredible honor serving under you on this mission, Commander." She reluctantly let go of his hand.

Chad resisted the urge to reach out and pull her toward him, instead he said, "It was because of your skill set, and that of the others on our team, that this mission was a success. It was my privilege to have you and your two assistants on my team."

Two of the male sharpshooters placed Jeff in a body bag and zipped it closed. Everyone on the team took a well-deserved break as together they waited for the Medevac that was on its way.

Cindy laid her head in Cara's lap and soon fell into an exhausted sleep, until the noise and wind of the rotors of the Medevac woke her up. She sat up and looked around herself in disoriented confusion, and then she looked up toward the sky and saw the helicopter hovering over them, looking for the best location to set down. She started crying uncontrollably and Cara and Stella wrapped their arms around her. Cindy sobbed into Stella's hair, "I thought it was all a dream that I had been saved! Thank all of you, and thank God it is real! I'm really going home."

After the helicopter set down, the paramedic loaded Cindy on board and immediately started her on an IV drip, while a couple of the male sharpshooters helped strap Jeff's corpse onto the rockers of the helicopter.

Together, Chad and his team watched the Medevac lift off with Cindy and her attacker on board. Everyone on the ground had smiles on their faces, although this was a bittersweet moment for them all. The team then turned and started back down the mountain.

Chapter 12

A week later, back in the town of Elk, Chad sat on a chair in the hospital room where Randy was recovering from the gunshot wound, which he had received from his brother. Two armed guards stood outside the door. In the room with Chad was the Police Chief of Elk, who was there to serve as a witness more than anything else. Chad turned on his voice recorder before he began his last interrogation of Randy.

Chad said, "Randy, we have recovered all of the missing girl's bodies, which were buried at the cabin in the woods. However, there is another body of a female, which we have been unable to identify. Would you care to share with us whom she was, so we can notify her family? She is of Asian or Native American ancestry."

Randy frowned and said, "She was a prostitute. She was hitchhiking when Jeff and I picked her up. She was trying to make her way up to Canada, because she had some relatives there she was going to try to find. She said that she was lured to the United States with the false promise of a modeling career, but, when they smuggled her here, they took her passport and forced her into prostitution."

"So, she was from somewhere in Asia? Do you happen to know what her name was?"

"Yeah, she was Chinese. She called herself Cherry, and that is all I know."

"Did she have any kind of identification on her, or perhaps an address of any of her relatives?" Chad asked.

"No, because she said that she escaped with just basically the clothes on her back. She offered to have sex with us for money, to help on her journey."

"Then why did you two kill her?"

Randy stiffened and became defensive, "I told you that I have never killed anyone!"

"OK, then why did Jeff kill her?"

"Well, first off, we didn't have any damned money, and besides that, Jeff wouldn't have given her any money if we did have it, and lastly, because Jeff enjoyed killing the girls."

"Are there any other girls out there that we did not find yet? And, Randy, you need to be fully aware that if you lie to us about this, and we find another victim, your plea deal could be off the table. And the people in this state and the next one over are going to want your head on a platter. Do I make myself perfectly clear? Chad said.

"There are not any others."

Chad posed his next question, "Randy, what was the ten thousand dollars for?"

"It was for Cindy."

"What do you mean that it was for Cindy?" Chad asked.

"The money was for Cindy, because she was different than the other girls."

"What do you mean that she was different from the other girls?"

"She was a paid hit, but I swear to you that I didn't know anything about that. Jeff tricked me into helping him kidnap her. The night that we robbed Porter's Stop and Go, I thought it was going to be a simple robbery. I didn't even know anything about the hit, until I found the money in Jeff's backpack. I thought he took the girl for the same reason that he took the others. I begged him to leave her there, but he refused."

Chad leaned back in his chair, folded his arms, and asked, "Then why did you help him abduct her, Randy?"

"Are you kidding me? We had just pulled an armed robbery, so it was not like I had time to stand around and argue with Jeff. We needed to get the hell out of there!"

"Who paid you the money, Randy?"

"Like I told you, no one paid me the money. I accidently found it in Jeff's backpack. He was holding out on me, and then he tried to sucker me into making the hit, even though I knew nothing about it."

"Who paid Jeff the ten thousand dollars to kill Cindy, Randy?"

"Mrs. Porter paid Jeff the money."

Surprised by the answer Chad leaned forward and said, "Her mother paid Jeff to kill her own daughter?"

Randy shook his head, "No, it was the old bitch that Jeff said paid him the money to kill her granddaughter. We had set some businesses on fire for her, and a couple of old houses too. So I guess she felt that we were the ones for this job too."

"She paid you two to set fire to her businesses?"

"Yeah, she did. But she also paid us to burn some other businesses too."

"Was that to throw off her insurance company?" Chad asked.

Randy shrugged and said, "Who knows, I don't have a clue what her intent was, but that sounds about right."

Chad stood up and said, "Thank you for the information, Randy." And together, he and the Elk Police Chief walked out of the hospital room.

In the corridor of the hospital, the police chief said, "It sounds like the old woman was strapped for cash. And here everyone thought that she was one of the richest people around. Do you think that you have enough on her to bring her in?"

"I will just as soon as I get our auditing team on it." Chad called Dan.

Dan answered his phone, "Adams speaking."

"Dan this is Turner here. We need a full scale audit of Mrs. Porter Sr.'s bank records. And time is of the essence."

"It is a damn audit, Turner. Why is an audit so damned critical?"

"It is critical, because we need more evidence to make an arrest for arson and attempted murder for financial gain."

Dan let out a long sigh, and said, "Alright, I'm calling the audit department right now."

Finally, Chad received the audit of all Mrs. Porter Sr.'s banking transactions. From the audit, it was obvious that funds were being moved from one business to prop up the books of her other businesses, and so it went with her business that continued to bleed red. She had played this shell game for so long that it eventually affected her few businesses she owned which had books that were still in the black, because she kept bleeding their profits to keep her failing businesses afloat.

Chad wondered why she didn't just simply sell the failing businesses and cut her losses. And then he thought about what George, the desk clerk at Porter's Inn, had told him about Mrs. Porter Sr.'s humble beginnings. She had built a small empire all on her own and, sadly, it had become more important to her than her own flesh and blood. Her empire was crumbling and apparently she would stop at nothing to try and save it. In Chad's world, he saw criminals who put material items and money above human life far too often.

At first, she turned to arson, because she could recoup her loses for those failed businesses with the books that she had cooked. She also had the few remaining dilapidated rentals that she still owned torched, and it apparently didn't matter to her if they were occupied or not. She collected the insurance money for those, but never rebuilt, although she did retain ownership of the newly bare lots, because it seemed that Mrs. Porter Sr. had issues with letting go of these inanimate objects. However, she apparently had no problem sacrificing her granddaughter to try to save her empire. She may very well have gotten away with her scheme, if she had not, unbeknownst to her, hired the serial killers that Chad had set out to find.

As the evidence began to flow in, and with Mrs. Porter Sr. under interrogation, her story about a prowler at her residence the night of Cindy's abduction began to unravel. It soon became apparent that she called in a false report to redirect the usual patrol of Porter's Stop and Go to her residence, so that Cindy's abduction could occur.

Please write a review on Amazon.com. It will be greatly appreciated.

Made in the USA
Lexington, KY
11 February 2019